漱石の名作に恋して

江上 信行

まえがき

　夏目漱石は江戸生まれの東京育ち、江戸っ子の漱石は七年間、他の所、暮らしをしている。

　転勤等で赴いた松山、熊本、ロンドンである。

　他の所生活の苦労や気遣いもあったようだ。新婚生活の所、子供が生まれた所、景色がきれいだった所、お隣さんが良かった所、良い出会いがあった所など、離れた後でそのことを述べている。生まれ故郷の江戸東京が一番であったろうが、そのような因縁で他所も愛着が湧いたのだろう。それら精神的にも得た多くの世界は、漱石の自らの作品に反映されている。

　その世界は、漱石作品を読み始めた青春時代の私の心に響いた。

　私を、四角な世界から常識と名のつく一角を磨減した、三角の芸術の世界へ導いてくれた。そして又、母がいる故郷のなつかしい世界と、学問の世界と、美しい女性が燦として春の如くある社交の世界の、三つの世界へも導いてくれた。

　体力だけを備えた無学で無知なそれまでの私を論してくれたのである。

　この『漱石の名作に恋して』では、漱石の代表的な作品のタイトルを文章の中へ散りばめた。

　無理矢理な個所もあるが、漱石との楽しい時間の世界を遊んだ。

3

目次

一

バタパタバタパタ、ブルーン、ブルーン、

ゴーゴー、ゴーゴー、ザー、ザー、ガーガー

エンジンタービンとプロペラ回転の合体した音が鳴り響き耳を突く。その音と共に生じる強い風が丸めた体を揺らし押し付ける。周囲の深草もいっしょに音頭を取るように騒ぎ立て生きがる。春であるが二百十日の野分の様だ。HU1Bヘリコプターは大草原の演習場に着陸すると、飛んでいた時とは違う急変した。それまで遊覧飛行のような気分にさせていたこのヘリコプターは、江画嶋たちが訓練状況に入り、外に出た瞬間から昨今のニュース映像で知るベトナムの戦場を飛び回るあのヘリコプターを想像させるように気取りだした。着陸しても緊急に飛び立てる態勢で身構え、余計に荒立っている。

「江画嶋、藤原、いいか――、行動開始」

多重無線通信班の第一組の組長、中村二曹はこれらの強騒音に負けないぐらいの大声を出したが、半分以上はかき消されて虫のかすれた鳴き声のようだ。

「はい、了解でーす」

精一杯の返事は組員自身の耳にも入らない。三人は搭載させていた相当の量の通信資器材を降ろしながら一斉にプロペラ回転円の外位置に集積していった。

黒々とした雲が覆いかぶさる空からは、雨も疑似戦場の舞台造りに参加して来た。

「こらー、休むな、気合、気合、急げーえー」

「こらー、二台目、いち、にいー、さあーん、発電機二号、よーし」

「発電機一号、よーし、いち、にいー、さーん」

「重いぞ、気合を入れよー、いち、にいー、さーん」

「アンテナエレメント、よし、搬送端局装置、よし、多重無線機、よし、発電機一号」

「こらー、気合が足らんぞ、ふたりとも飯は食べたのかー、急げ、急げ」

「今日は、あ、今晩は、コーヒー一緒していいですか」

「あら、江画嶋、君も休講?」

「いいえ、遅くなっただけです。美人先輩は休講のことを知っていたのですか」

「美人? まあー本当の事を言っていただいてありがとう。知らなかったのよ、休講のこと」

「そうですか」

「前時限に間に合うように普通に来たの、先生の急な用事だから仕方がないわ」

「だから最初からここにいたのですね。僕もここにいよう」

「君はだめだよ、遅刻でも講義を聴きに行きなさい、もったいないよ」

「いえ、まだ二回目の授業だからいいでしょう。もう四〇分も経っているし」

「そこのところが重要よ」

「美人先輩も厳しいなー」

「まあいいでしょう。コーヒー、一緒してあげる、仕方なく」

「大先輩から言われればまあまあ、少しうれしいですよ、二歳年上のおっかさんからでも、あ、いや、び、美人から」

「こらっ、だけど江画嶋はいいな、授業開始の時間には遅れずに確実に来ることができる職場だから。私なんか忙しい時はそうはいかないわ、代りもいないし、今日はやっと早く来ることができて、来てみたらこういうこと」

「そんなことないですよ、僕も訓練、演習のときはまったく来ることができません。昨日がそうでした。今日の昼過ぎに山から帰って来たのです。とりあえずの整備が終わり、やっと来ることができました」

「君もそうなんだ。じゃあ、お互いやっと来たということね」

大学敷地内にある木々の真新しい葉が夕陽に照らされている。純色の若葉群は真横からの光源でコントラスを強く鮮やかにしてみずみずしく光っている。

その中に同時に映えている白壁で、平屋造りの小奇麗な建物が大学喫茶部である。内部は飾り気のない質素で清潔な雰囲気で、いつも学生の希望の音楽が流れる。外の景色のように、入学したての希望溢れる新鮮な表情が充満している。

今日は第二部（夜間部）の前時限目授業中の時間にしては空き椅子はほとんど無い。ある科目の急な休講でその履修者たちが、次の時間を待って多く利用していたのだ。本来、休講は熱心に学ぶ学生に対して良いことではないのであるが、第二部の学生たちにとっては少し

8

別の意味も持っていた。午後六時から七時三〇分の九〇分間の休講時間は昼の仕事の疲れを癒す絶好のものでもあったからだ。流れているポピュラー音楽はその癒しに程良く手伝っていた。あわよくば、午後七時四〇分から九時一〇分までの後時限の科目も休講であったなら、と贅沢も思ってみたかった。

「江画嶋、良く聞いて、第二部の学生は勤労通学者ということで二つの世界があるの。昼の働く職場は現実的社会人としての世界であり、夜は理想人として真理の追求にいそしむ勉学の世界よ。偉そうに言うけど、この二つを若い時に同時に経験することは幸せなことだよ。こんなことは職場での配慮がなければ不可能なことで、忙しいときも仕事から通常時間に引ける恩に報いるには授業の出席だけがそれに応えることなの。でもね、日々欠席しない努力は当然必要であり、少しは堅苦しいと思うこともあるけど。だからさあー、みんなこの休講は正当な理屈付けにはもってこいの休み時間であり、仕事の疲労を引きずりながら夜間に学ぶ者にとっては有り難い時間、と思うよ」

「えーと、美人先輩が言いたい本音を簡単に訳すれば、ときには休講もあったほうがいい、ということでしょう」

「簡単に言えばそうなの、この時間に、持ってきたこの文庫本を読むことも出来るし」

「次の文学の予習にもなりますね、さすがー、ぼくも真面目に買って来ました。かさ張らないから文庫がいいですね。小さくて安くもあるし、全集は次の段階ですね」

「君も読みなさい」

「少しは読んで来ました。さん、しろー」

「どれくらい読んだの」

「二ページぐらい」

「君ー、それくらいで解かったの」

「はい、柔道の物語ではないようです。姿三四郎では」

「あのねー、夏目漱石に関しては私が少しはましなようね」

「ぼっちゃんと、わがはいはねこであーる、ぐらいは知っていましたが、その他の題名は全く知りませんでした。美人先輩はどれくらい知っていたのですか」

「夏目漱石は熊本に四年間滞在したと先週習ったでしょう。それくらいは前から知っていたの、だからねー、熊本と漱石の関係に興味はあったの、一般教養科目で文学を専攻したのもそのためよ。くさまくら、にひゃくとうか、も熊本に関係があるから君もよく読んで勉強しなさい。私は漱石熊本三部作と名付けているの」

「さすが、幼稚園、小学校、中学校、高校の大先輩、頼りがいがありますね。美人先輩と一緒に受ける唯一つの授業ですから張り切っていきます」

「君ー、大先輩や美人はやめてくれない？」

「遠慮しなくていいですよ。タダにしておきますから」

「かわいい後輩からだから仕方がないか、まあ、有り難くその呼び方に従うわ」

「そうでなくちゃー。ところで前回、蒲池先生は小説の文章を一人ずつ読んでもらうと言っ

ていましたが、漢字の読み方を間違ったら恥ずかしいですね」

「気にしなくていいよ、君には当たらないから」

「そうでしょうか？　人気の科目で人が多いからですか」

「それもあるけど読めそうな人にしか先生は指名しないよ」

「それじゃー僕の顔は…」

喫茶部の窓から見える外の様子は宵の近づきを感じさせてきた。彼岸過迄とはいわず、入学する四月も天候によってその日の夕方の明るさが異なる。晴れの日と、曇り、雨の日では極端である。五月、六月と月が経つにつれてこの差は小さくなり、夏季休講に入るまでの前時限の授業は明るい窓の中で終始する。後期の前時限の時は、また、明るさがまちまちになる。そして晩秋からは前時限の授業が始まる時にはすでに完全な夜間部である。

このような季節の変化を敏感に感じながらの、毎日二時限、三時間の学生生活である。前時限、後時限のあいだ一〇分の休み時間はだいたい他の講義室への移動時間になる。

これらの慌ただしい時間が終了してキャンパスの門を出る時は数分もしないうちに気持と体は次の日の仕事に備えるためのものになる。

必然、二部の学生は限られた時間に学生相互の会話を作り出す努力、それが価値の対象であり希望で、また楽しみになる。

「美人先輩、３３３号講義室が待っています。夏目漱石に会いに行きましょう」

「時間だね、吾輩は美人猫である、どお？」

３３３講義室はすでに履修者でいっぱいだった。一般教養科目の文学は女子学生の受講が多く、他の科目に比べて男子との割合がここだけは極端に逆転していた。江画嶋の同僚などは他の科目を選んでいた。

　先週に行なわれた初めての講義では、文学を今後の人生にどう生かすか、また、その取り組み方などが主なものだった。その中心となる夏目漱石と熊本の関係の概要が話され、今日から数回は『三四郎』についての読釈が行われることになっていた。

「君はあの付近に座りなさい」

「あそこは女性ばっかりじゃないですか、美人先輩は？」

「私はあの同学年の隣に座るわ」

「ぼくも後ろの方がいいなー」

「だめだよ、若い人は前、前、良い事があるかもよー」

「前の席の人から読まされたりすることですか」

「そうじゃないの」

　江画嶋は先輩の言う事を聞いて渋々前の方に席を取った。主に男子学生と席を並べる他の科目と違って自分が浮いた存在に感じたが、一方では女性を避ける席を選ぼうにも選べられないことを妙に喜んでいる自分もあった。教壇に向かって、前から三列目、中通路の右側、一番内の席、前の方はその席しか空いていなかったのだ。教壇からは見れば真ん中になる。その空いている席に座った。そして、ノートと文

庫本の『三四郎』を机上に置いて周りを少しだけ見回した。軽い圧力を感じ、あまり良くない席に座ったと思った。すぐに首と体を動かし後方の席を見た。一番うしろの席、中通路の左側、内から一番目の席では、同学年と聞いた横の席の学生と、楽しそうに語っている女先輩の顔が見えた。

江画嶋は語り合っている二人は物語などのヒーロー、ヒロインとしては絶対に登場しないような二人だと軽々しい思いを遊んだ。遊びながら、マンガ雑誌や映画にしか興味がなく空想ばかりしていた今までの自分を振り返った。江画嶋は小説を読むことなど面倒臭いもので、生きて行くための生活には必要のない代物と感じていた。

当然、男性組織の直感的荒々しい雰囲気のなかで仕事をしている江画嶋には、これから始まる文学にたいして何も感じるものや、思い出す事などなく、単位取得の一科目という意識だった。

蒲池教授が講義室に入り黒板の前に立った。手に持っていた分厚い全集本を檀上の机に置き、軽く一礼をした。騒めいていた講義室が静かになった。教授は話を始めるまで数秒の間を置いた。履修者は一斉に注視し、初一言に耳を傾けた。空気の波が停止して、点灯している蛍光灯の波長音が聞こえそうだ。

「みなさん、息はしていますか」

その瞬間、ドッと笑い声が渦巻いた。

一気に講義の内に入った坐り人は、その後すぐに教授の老巧な話術により夏目漱石の世界

へ引きずり込まれていった。

〈うとうとして眼が覚めると女は何時の間にか、隣の爺さんと話を始めている。・・・・・、女とは京都からの相乗である〉

講義が進んでいく途中に教授自ら『三四郎』の導入部分を読み始めた。聴講のすべての眼は檀上から紙上の活字に一気に移った。

〈・・・、乗った時から三四郎の眼に着いた。第一色が黒い。三四郎は九州から山陽線に移って、女の色が次第に白くなるので何時の間にか故郷を遠退くような憐れを感じていた。それでこの女が車室に這入って来た時は、何となく異性の味方を得た心持がした。この女の色は実際九州色であった〉

ここで文章朗読を止めた蒲池教授は、次の男と女の宿での絡みの場面からは落語仕立てで話し出した。その中で主人公の三四郎を紹介するくだりを面白く可笑しく語る途中に、今度は、いきなり右人差し指を構え、ズーと狙いを定めてサッとその右腕を伸ばした。

「君、女性群の花園の中にいる男子君、さよならの場面のところから読んで下さい。大きな声で、ですよ」

江画嶋は仰天した。仰天しながら周りを見た。確認した。さすがに近くの席の男性は江画嶋だけだった。先生の目と人差し指は江画嶋を鋭く刺していた。また、周りを見た。にたり顔、したり顔、慰め顔、百面の顔で前の者は振り返り、左右の者は首を出し、江画嶋を覗

14

く。講義室全体が小さく騒めいた。小学生の頃から立って声を出して読むのをあまり好きで

はなかった江画嶋は、ここは覚悟を決めた。読み手第一号で記念すべき代表であることを喜

ぶ、と自分自身に言い聞かせた。だが困った。どのような調子で読めばいいか迷った。昼の

仕事では大声を出すことを常とし、端正さを要求される。そんな雰囲気で読むのか、そうか

といってそれは刺刺しい。だが不慣れな弱い声では調子が狂うだろう。とにかく腰を椅子か

ら外しその場に立った。後方の二人から拍手が来た。それに連られる様に江画嶋の周囲の

多くからも拍手が出た。開いている文庫本の厚い冊の方を左手で握り、右手は親指と人差し

指、中指で薄い方のページ冊を軽く挟み添えた。

「皆さん今年度最初の名朗読です。静かに、静かにして聞きましょう」

教授のことばに今度もドッと沸いた。江画嶋はそれが静まり返ってから努めてゆっくり、

はっきりと読み始めた。いつかはこのような読む番が来るとは思っていたが、いきなりとは

驚いた。文章に出てくる漢字の読み方の予習は全くしていない。何しろ解説の部分をパラパ

ラと目を通していただけだった。実のところ大きな声で読む自信はなかった。先生に聞こえ

る程度でいいだろうと考えた。「ああ、なんという度胸の無さだ。声が揺れる。これくらい

の事で、落ち着け、落ち着け」

〈・・・・停車場へ着いた時、女は関西線で四日市の方へ行くのだと

云うことを三四郎に話した。三四郎の汽車は間もなく来た。時間の都

合で女は少し待ち合わせる事となった。改札場の際まで送って来た女

は、

「色々御厄介になりまして、・・・・・では御機嫌よう」と丁寧に御辞儀をした。三四郎は革鞄と傘を片手に持ったまま、空いた手で例の古帽子を取って、只一言、「さよなら」と云った。女はその顔を、、、、、、、、、、、、、と眺めていた、が〉

横から「まじまじと」と教える声が聞こえた。江画嶋は〈女はその顔を〉から読み直した。

〈女はその顔を凝と眺めていた、が、やがて落着いた調子で「あなたは余っ程度胸のない方ですね」と云って、にやりと笑った。三四郎はプラット、フォームの上へ弾きだされた様な心持がした。やが・・・〉

「はい、そこまでー」

江画嶋は教授の声で読むのを止めた。大役を成し遂げたような安堵感がした。

「まあまあ良かったですね、君が主人公みたいだったよ」

またドッと来た。江画嶋は妙な気持になった。そして、たかが読むだけのことで僅かな興奮を覚える我を嘆いた。教授の話は続いていたが一瞬だけ集中出来ずにいた。すぐに我を取り戻し、顔を半分動かして横目で、読み方を教えてくれた隣を見た。隣の女子学生は熱心に前の方を向いているだけだった。

講義が終わり一斉にみんなが動き出した。江画嶋はすぐに首を右に向けた。隣は先隣りの者と話しながらすぐに席を離れた。

漱石の名作に恋して　一

二

野外発電機は鈍い回転音を発して三千六百回転の正常な動きに達せず停止する。十数回、起動紐を回転歯車に掛け引いても起動しない。

「田中士長だめです。起動しません」

「点火プラグをあと一回磨け」

「供用品は図太いから扱いにくいですね」

「なにを言っているか、お前の紐を引く力が弱いから回らないんだ。どれ、俺がやる」

ドッ、ドッ、ドドドド、バッ、バッ、ババババーバー

「さすがー、飯の数がちがいますね」

「江画嶋、感心するなー、ぼぉーとしていないで電圧、出力点検を早くやれ」

「は、はい」

「何事か、二人とも。早くしないと電波発射の時間に間に合わないぞ」

「花田一曹、心配いりません、自局調整もスムーズに完了していまーす」

「そうか、中継の山崎三曹も準備完了して電波を出せる状態だ。周波数も間違いないか」

「はい、確認、終っています」

「よし、電波、発射」

18

「発射します」

「受信レベルよし、感度良好です。B端と中継の間も感度良好だそうです。B端と回線調整を実施します」

田中と江画嶋は素早く、数分間で相手局との無線区間レベル調整と端末信号通話試験を終わらせた。田中は通信所シェルター内から、外で指揮を執っている花田一曹に大きな声で報告した。

「全チャンネル異常なし、構成完了しました。SN比も良好です」

「よーし、中村二曹のルートも終わっているそうだ。五分後にこの縮小系は全回線閉所撤収、撤収後、器材庫に集合、次の演習本番の説明を行う」

田中が江画嶋に笑い顔で言った。

「江画嶋、今日は通常通り大学に行かれるぞ」

「ありがとうございます。田中士長のお蔭です」

「こらー、そうじゃない。お前の頑張りもあったからだ」

夕刻の大学前バス停はバスの停車時間が長くなる。普段でも通勤通学者のバスは満員であるが、二部学生が降りる時間帯は受講終了の昼の学生が乗車するときと重なり特に混雑する。

別ルートからのバスもいっしょに停車し並ぶ。

仕事を終え、満員の中を揺られて乗っていた社会人は、バスから出た瞬間に外の空気に触

れて身心の軽さを感じ、すぐの大学入り口正門へ入る。正門は背丈よりも少し低い左右の石造り門柱になっていて、左には短大名、右には大学名が書かれている。門柱と門柱の幅より広い道幅は十五、六メートル、その幅で両側には整然と銀杏の木が植えられている。社会人はその並木道を進み、受講を終えた昼間の学生と行き交いながら自分達も学生に変身していく。

多くの大学施設は端然と十分にして、それらの人の気持ちを包むように誘い待ち構えている。並木道の突き当り真正面には両側の並木を威張って監視しているようにドンと構えている一本の王様格の銀杏の木がある。そのすぐ後ろに二階建て五号館側面の壁がその一本の木の引立て役となっている。ざらざらしたセメント壁で、くすんだ色合いは建物の古さを感じさせる。この二つがここから左右に分かれている大学道の基点だ。

基点を右へ進む。

講義棟が連なる学内唯一の舗装道、メインストリートと呼んでもいいがその道へと入って行くことになる。道の右側に解体されようとしている古い体育館が見えて来るが、すでに新しい体育館の建設準備が進んでいる。

そこから先は順に四階建の四号館、三階建の一号館、そして二号館の図書館になる。道を挟んだ四号館前は樹木が多く、記念館、喫茶、売店があり、憩の区域だ。

図書館左手前に平屋の大講堂があり、大講堂から伸びた屋根の下にはロビーが造られている。そのロビーは、一号館左側一階出入り口も結んでいる。ロビーには屋内掲示板が備え付ける。

けられている。

奥に四階建ての三号館がある。その一階部分は学生食堂である。一号館二階、三号館二階、図書館二階閲覧室の三か所はモダンなブリッジと言われる通路で結ばれていて、お互いの玄関口に降りなくても行き来が可能だ。

ブリッジ下は四つの建物の一階部分通路として利用出来るようになっているので、その中心拠点がロビーということになる。江画嶋は出逢いロビーと名を付けた。

この一帯がキャンパスの中心施設群で、大学本部がある一号館の前はロータリーとした小綺麗な円庭と三角庭がある。

陸上競技や野球、バレーなどが総合的に実施出来る大きいグラウンドは、これらの施設群前のメインストリートを挟んですぐ全面に広がり、敷地を囲んでいるポプラの並木をパノラマ的に望むことが出来る。

基点を左へ進む。

五号館とまったく同じ二階建ての古い講義棟が左に二棟並行して建っている。六号館、七号館と呼ばれている。その奥に第二体育館、右手前に高飛び込み台が付いているプール、三面のテニスコートがある。

社会人通学者はこのような広いキャンパス内での大学生時間を、自由空間修養時間として捉えることも常に意識していた。

江画島は同僚二人と一緒にバスから降りた。三人は各自五歩ぐらいの間隔をとって歩き、

数十秒の時間差で出逢いロビーの掲示板前に着いた。後時限に行なわれる体育の、はじめての実技の予定が記されている掲示板を見ながら同僚たちは言った。「昼間にタップリと体を使っているから体育など受けなくてもいいのにな—」と。江画嶋も思った。「仕方がない、必須科目だから」と言いながら掲示板を恨めしそうに見流した。体育実技は第二体育館での授業である。この第二体育館は、狭く暗く、直系一メートルはある円形のコンクリート柱六本が空間を奪っている。軍事施設と言った方がいいようなもので、ここに体育資材が置いてある。新しい体育館が完成するまで屋内での体育実技が行われていた。実技種目によっては不向きなようだが、創意工夫で学生が納得する良い授業を目指すと講師は伝えていた。

三号館での前時限を終えた江画嶋はまた出逢いロビーに来た。江画嶋が尊敬と親しみを抱いている女先輩がいた。

その女先輩は江画嶋の二歳年上である。高校時代は担任の先生から大学進学を勧められていたが家庭の状況で仕方なく断念し卒業後すぐに働き出した。だが四年が過ぎて再び沸いてきた学びの気持が夜間の大学に通わせていると言う。江画嶋もまた入隊時の教育訓練や職場の異動などで機会がなく、同じ歳の現役生と三年遅れでの入学である。二人の現学年は一年違いとなる。

「江画嶋、次は何?」

「体育です」

「君は受けなくて返事だけしておけばいいんじゃないの、体はいつも鍛えているでしょう」

22

と冗談のように言った。江画嶋は物分りの善い人もいるものだと思いながら控えめに「体が資本の仕事ですが…」と言えば、「頭はどうでもいいのね」と単刀直入に返された。

「ええ、まあ、そうです」と答えた。

「うふっ、冗談を言ったけどごめんね、でも若い時はそれがいいかもしれない。この前言ったこととニュアンスは一緒だけど、若い君の理想はこうよ。昼の仕事で体を、夜の大学で頭を、どう、私の言うこと」

「さすが美人先輩、今日も素晴らしい言葉、ありがとうございます」

「目指すは文武両道、えーと、理文二刀、バランス、バランス」

「益々素晴らしいですね、大先輩は」

「明日また文学でよろしくね」

立ち話をした江画嶋は、急いで次の講義室に行く女先輩の後ろ姿を見詰めた。その女先輩は言動のはっきりした性格で、映画やテレビのドラマに出てくる気丈なおかあさん役にピッタリの風貌で、江画嶋を先導するにはもったいないほどの大きな先輩だった。その先輩から見れば江画嶋はなんでも聞いてくれる弟役である。実家を離れている二人が学内で会うことは故郷に会うことと同じであった。

第二体育館に向かう途中に同僚二名が追い掛けて来た。同じ駐屯地で働いているが職種の違う二人である。だが互いの仕事上の不平不満を話し合うことで気持の繋がりは出来ている同僚だ。同僚間の情報交換も早い。しかしその欠点も

23

あった。常に三人だけの世界になれば、昼の職場の延長の時間に成りかねないことだ。
大学で学ぶ三人の合言葉を、千差万別、として、この合言葉を大切な学びの原点に置いた。異なる価値観を知る絶好の大学生時間は、偏る意識の中和時間として位置付けることが通学者の取り柄であると入学直後に話し合っていた。そのために三人は確認の意図として、大学のキャンパス内では努めて行動を共にしないように、また同一科目受講の講義室では近い席に座らないと申し合わせていた。
二人は江画嶋の両脇に追い付いた。
「江画嶋君、体育館に行くときだけは群がろう」
「おお、新名君と松尾君、それがいいだろう」
三人が横に並んで歩き出した途端に意見も横並びに成立、次の週からも体育が始まる前と後は共同歩調を取ることとなった。江画嶋と同僚二人はクラス違いで、いつもの実技内容は異なるが、最初のこの日は同じ体力測定であった。
台の上り下り後の脈測り、体の柔軟性の測定、ジグザグドリブルなど江画嶋には軽かったが、日頃行わない動きに目新しさ感じた。女性も混ざったグループ毎に種目を済ませていく中で、互いの会話も徐々に増え、次第に楽しい体育実技となっていった。早く終ったグループは次の種目を待つ間、前グループの見学の時間となる。江画嶋も別グループを見ていた。
あの時、文学の時、漢字の読み方を横から教えてくれたあの女子学生が掛け声に合わせ、髪をなびかせて台の上り下りをしていた。出席取りの最初のときは全く気に掛けていなかっ

たが、その姿をしばらく見続けた。

後時限の体育が終わり、群れの三人は第二体育館を出た。第二体育館から正門までの経路は幾通りもあったが、ほとんどの者が当然のように来た道を逆に歩き、明るい四号館の前で右に曲がり正門に向かった。

「並木道を横隊行進だ」

三人は横に並んで王様銀杏木の前から歩調を数えて調子よく歩いた。

「百九十歩」

「松尾君、新名君、何メートルか答えなさい」

「はい、江画嶋大将、百三十三メートルであります」

三人は同時に笑った。

バス停に帰りのバスが着いた。

三

「こらー、追い越されるぞー、手を振れ、手を、あと少しだ、離れるなー」

江画嶋は必死になっていた。班リーダーの辻三曹から着合いを入れられても足が思い通りに動かない。体が重い。背納の紐が肩に食い込む。おまけに腹が痛くなってきた。昼飯の食べ過ぎだろうか。ゴールの駐屯地はまだ先だ。班対抗の武装持久走競争は、先に全員が到着した班が勝つ熾烈なもので、苦境に差しかかった。

通信の部隊も体力勝負である。五キロ先の標高百五十二メートルの立田山頂上往復のこの訓練は、班の名誉が掛かり必要以上に気力と気合を入れ張り切らなければならない。

低い山だが登りの途中からは狭い急な獣道を上らなければならない。緩やかな公園道を通ることは禁止だ。見晴展望所で道草を食うなどという戯けた計算は本末転倒で、頂上の三角点表を回って下り、住宅街も走り、走り続け、ライバルの四つの班は一人の脱落者も出さず駐屯地南門に辿り着いた。上司の村上三尉は江画嶋に言った。「良く頑張った。汗を拭いて次に備えなさい。夜の大学での勉強中には寝るなよ」と。

江画嶋が勤務する駐屯地の表門を出れば樹齢数十年の古い桜の木が連なる長い並木坂があ

26

並木は門の中から連なっているので花が満開のときは遠方鮮やかな坂になる。その坂を下り切ると、菊池電車の線路と、その線路と並行する道路に突き当る。江画嶋は電車の線路を跨いで道路脇のバス停からバスに乗り、広狭の混雑する地方道、国道、県道を進み、市電が走る道路に出てすぐの薬園町バス停で降りる。後ろは道路から一段高くなっている石垣積み、お寺敷地の境界である。石垣は高さも幅もあり、上にはその石垣を土台にした幾つもの映画の立て看板が同じ幅で取り付けられ、人目を引き寄せる役目で並んでいる。降りてからは百五十メートルほど歩いて大学経由があるバス停に行く。

辺りの界隈は、市電の始着点や市民の台所と呼ばれる子飼商店街があり、また学生の街として活気に溢れ大変に賑やかな雑踏である。田舎町出身の江画嶋はここでバスを待つ間に気持が引き締まり、仕事の疲れを忘れていく。

バスを乗り換えれば、そのバスはすぐのV字型交差点を右斜めに少し上りながら進み、楕円のアーチが架かった橋を渡りだすと川幅の空間で左右の眺めが開け、渡り切るところからは少し下りながら次の街並み入る。そこからバスは加速をつけるように一直線に学んでいる大学前まで走る。江画嶋が考えたこの、通い路は、次のような表現になった。

仕事の剛門を出て、活社会路を通り、それから学びの柔門へ。

〈三四郎がじっとして池の表を見詰めていると、大きな木が幾本となく木の底に映って、その又底に青い空が見える。三四郎はこの時電車よりも、東京よりも、日本よりも遠くかつ遥かな心持がした。・・・・・・・・・・・・・・・・

27

熊本の高等学校に居る時分もこれより静かな龍田山に上ったり・・・・〉

江画嶋は『三四郎』のこの一節で、自分が利用している乗り換えバス停の近くにある大学は三四郎が学んだ高等学校であったこと、また、その裏の龍田山が、いや、立田山がその小説に紹介されていることなどを知った。そのことで、今まで自分が無能で知識の無さ過ぎだったことを改めて感心した。

特に立田山は職場からも近く、愛すべき丘、いや、山だ。駆け足訓練で上ったりするが、漱石が上ったとなれば遥か昔の明治時代の立田山に思いをめぐらすこともしなければと、時代の行人気取りの真似事も考えた。

ある日の日曜日、一人で外出した江画嶋は立田山に上り、眺望が利く一番良い場所で、市内の遠方から近方に眼を移し、広がる黒瓦屋根群の中に、独自の高さと大きさを持つ二つの大学の建造物を地点して声を出した。

「文学や、あー漱石や、漱石や」

そよ風に吹かれ、居眠りもした江画嶋は道を下る途中、紫色が混ざったような紅色のヒナゲシの花を見た。そう、虞美人草を。

四

「杭は十分大地に打ち付けてあるかー、ポールの繋ぎは確実か、支線の取り付け位置は良い
かー、アンテナエレメント組み立てと偏波は良いかー、接続ケーブル先端に緩みは無いか」

「準備完了です」

「了解、建柱！」

「こらー、斜めに上がっているぞー、用心せよー」

鉄ハンマーで打ちつけた数本の鉄杭、幾重にも組み合わされた鉄パイプ、蜘蛛の巣のよう
な支線の編み、地上に準備された送信用と受信用の通信塔二本が大空に向かって高く立ち上
がろうとしている。

　　　　　ドォーン、ビョーン

「一本目よし。二本目建柱」

　　　　　ドォーン、ビュビューン

「建柱よーし、傾き修正を実施します」

「よろしい」

「傾き修正よし、方向修正よし、アンテナ建柱終わり」

29

指導中の小隊長青木三尉の顔は厳しかった。

「遅い、何十分かかるんだ、基本動作も成っていない、直ちに撤収、それから休憩だ。その後再び建柱訓練を行う」

「分かりました」

組長の島山三曹は汗諾々の顔で組員に怒鳴った。

「撤収開始し、し、し」と投げやり気分に。

江画嶋も声を張り上げ歌い出した。

「ハアーーイ、大きな、おーきな空に、そおーらにアンテーナ建てて、たーてーてー」

三回目の文学講義は前時限の講義が休み時間に少し食い込んだので、始まる寸前に講義室に入った。今日もいっぱいで後方の空いている席に座った。始まってから一〇分もしないうちに何人かが指名されて読み進めた。

〈不図眼を上げると、左手の岡の上に女が二人立っている。女のすぐ下が池で、池の向う側が高い崖の木立で、その後が派手な赤煉瓦のゴシック風の建物である。そうして落ちかかった日が、凡ての向うから横に光を透してくる。女はこの夕日に向いて立っていた。三四郎のしゃがんでいる低い陰から見ると・・・・・〉

江画嶋の眼は活字から離れて、前回座った前の方の席へ向いた。瞬きを二回ぐらいしてか

ら、また活字に戻った。

〈二人は申し合わせた様に用のない歩き方をして、坂を下りてくる。・・・
・・・・・左の手に白い小さな花を持って、それを嗅ぎながら来
る。嗅ぎながら、鼻の下に宛がった花を見ながら、歩くので、眼は伏せ
ている。それで三四郎から一間ばかりの所へ来てひょいと留まった。
・・・・・・・と云いながら、仰向いた顔を元へ戻す、その拍子
に三四郎を一目見た。三四郎は慥に女の黒眼の動く刹那を意識した。〉

予読をしていない江画嶋の手は、江画嶋の顔に僅かに本を引き付けた。

〈・・二人の女は三四郎の前を通り過ぎる。若い方が今まで嗅いでいた白
い花を三四郎前へ落して行った。三四郎は二人の後姿を凝と見詰めてい
た。看護婦は先へ行く。若い方が後から行く。華やかな色の中に、白い
薄を染め抜いた帯が見える。頭にも真白な薔薇を一つ挿している。その
薔薇が椎の木陰の下の、黒い髪の中で際立って光っていた。〉

「どうです。皆さん、これが三四郎と美禰子の最初の出会いです。これを起点として物語が
発展していくのです。この二人の場面と、明治という時代の背景を中心にこれからの講義を
進めます。あーあ、もう一度、私も若くなりたい」

教授の話に、それまで静まり返った空気が一瞬のうちに賑やかになった。

「ここからしばらく二人は会いません。上手い作家はここで焦らすのです。いつ会うか、い

31

つ会うか、回りに回って別のことを書いていきます。その他の登場人物や、周りの街の様子などです。たとえば電車のことや…」

江画嶋は中学一年生の時の秋に、自分たちだけで初めて電車に乗った時を思い出した。国鉄熊本駅前から乗ったのだが、デパートに行くためにどこで降りればいいか分からず、慌てた友達が「デパートに行きたいからそこで降ろしてください」と大きな声で言ったので乗っている他のお客さんから笑われたことなどだ。その時は再建されてすぐの真新しい熊本城天守閣にも登った。電車が通り、城がある憧れの街、その街にある大学で学んでいることを思い深め自慢悦した。

《学年は九月十一日に始まった。三四郎は正直に午前十時半頃学校へ・・

・・・

「どうです。この小説の頃は秋入学だったんですよ日本も。良く読めばそういうところも面白いですね、男女関係だけじゃなく。ここからいろいろの出来事を入れ、焦らしていくのです。ところどころ読みながら話していきます。」

〈・・又しゃがんだ。あの女がもう一遍通れば可い位に考えて、度々岡の上を眺めたが、岡の上には人影もしなかった。・・・・・・・三四郎はもう帰るべき時間だと考えた〉

「来週の講義は二人の関係から離れ、熊本時代の漱石と俳句について述べたいと思います。漱石を学作った俳句の数の四十パーセント、九百五十五句を熊本時代に作っているのです。漱石を学

ぶ上でこれも重要なものです。再来週に二人が再会するところから始めましょう」

江画嶋は本をたたみ、すぐ廊下に出て女先輩を待った。女先輩はなかなか廊下に出て来なかった。まだあの同学年と話し込んでいた。待つ間にあの読みを教えてくれた女子学生が、他の者と話しながら出て来て前を通って行った。そのとき横から声がした。

「江画嶋先輩、なにを見ているのですか」

仕方なくその男の声の方を躊躇しながら向いた。文学は専攻していない後輩の大山だった。地元に残り、親の大工の手伝いをしながら地元から汽車とバスで通学している。この時間は隣の講義室で受けていた。

「ああ、大山、大先輩を待っているところだよ」

「あの大先輩、中学、高校と物凄く優秀だったそうですよ。担任の先生が女医さんを目指せと言っていたみたいですよ。顔と一致しませんね」

「うん、そう言っておく、大山がなんとかと」

「やめてください、三人の仲ですから。僕も文学を専攻すればよかった、三人で並んで受ければ楽しかったでしょうね」

「そうだな、なんでも教えてくれるし、年の功だな」

「そういえば上は四十歳代から下は十八、十九歳の幅広さは二部学生の特徴ですね。お互い友だちになれば、いい意味で絶好の勉強のチャンスですね。幸せなことですよ」

「そんなことを考えれば、なんと贅沢な環境だ。後輩からでも教えられるなー」

「でも江画嶋先輩、あの大先輩に年齢のことなど言ってはだめですよ」

「そういうことは解かるよ、オレも年寄りの部類だから」

二、三分の立ち話中に女先輩が廊下に出てきた。後輩二人が揃っているのを見て余程うれしかったのか、明るい顔で右手を大きく上げた。

「恋の予感、愛の予感、おもしろいねー君たち」

「大先輩、何事ですかそれ」

大山が驚いて言った。

「なあに美人先輩は小説のことをいっているだけだよ」

「江画嶋先輩、僕もやっぱり文学を選べばよかったなー」

三人は三号館を出て出逢いロビーに来た。夜に学ぶために考慮設置されている昼光色の照明それだけでなく、人が集まり行き来してはなやかな明るさが助長する。その出逢いロビーは、学業を終え帰路に着く前のひと時の場でもあった。そして連れ添い帰る起点でもあった。

「休講の予定、えーと、無い、あーあ残念至極」

掲示板を見て先輩のおどけた様子に後輩たちは顔を見合わせ笑った。出逢いロビーを出れば、講義を聴き終えた者が一斉に出てくる学内メインストリートを揃い歩く。右側に広がっているグラウンドの奥は闇に包まれているが手前の水捌け部分の一帯ははっきりとしている。

両脇を固めた江画嶋と大山は、真ん中で喋りながら歩く先輩の話に耳をかたむけながら歩いた。

急ぎ足で歩く者、ゆっくり語りながら歩く者、いずれにしても大勢向かっているのは

「君たち、この帰る時間が一番充実を感じるときじゃないかしら。仕事を済ませ、勉強も済ませ、一日をたっぷり過ごしたことの満足を覚えるでしょう」

「そういえばそうですね、息をするような暇もなく」

「江画嶋、それは言い過ぎだけど、でもこれに満足するだけではだめだよ。青年期は将来の目標とそれを実行するための計画、それが大事なの。昼の学生は一生懸命に勉強して受験競争に打ち勝って入学しているの、君たちはあまりそうではなかったでしょう。ただ大学に通えばいいっていうものでもないの、せっかく来ているのだから、しっかりと勉強しなさい。教養を身に着けることは昼の仕事に生かすことにもなるの。上に立つ人は学歴だけでなくて、専門性と同時に幅広い知識も必要よ、どんな未来にも対応できるようにしておくことね。大山、君もだよ」

「大先輩、大工にもですか」

「あたりまえだよ。大工でなく建築家と自分で言いなさい。将来、弟子が出来て指導する立場になるわよ」

江画嶋、大山の二人は並木道を出ればすぐ左にある歩道橋を利用して道路の向かい側にあるバス停まで歩いた。帰りのときの乗車は降りるときの逆のバス停になる。女先輩は帰る方向が真反対であったので歩道橋は渡らず、江画嶋たちが来るときに降りるバス停から乗って行った。

並木道、正門そしてすぐのバス停がある通りだ。

江画嶋たちが乗るバスは上熊本駅行きのバスである。駐屯地に行くバスに乗り換えるために江画嶋は途中で降り、大山はそのまま駅まで行った。夏目漱石が熊本に第一歩を踏み出した駅だ。

五

〝 起床、起床 〞

ドタン、ドタン、ドタン

「これは訓練ではない。ただちに廊下に集合、営内班長は人員を掌握せよ」

「第二営内班、異常なし」「第一営内班、異…」

「よし、報告はよろしい、揃ったから連絡する。現在二時三〇分、当直司令より指示があった。先ほど他所で地震が有り、災害対処のため待機命令が出た。各職種の先任は班長が到着するまで指揮を執り、いつでも出発出来るように準備せよ。なお災害の規模、対処の期間、通信網など全く不明である。最大限の努力をせよ、解散」

江画嶋は大学から帰ってから、今先、眠入ったような感覚だった。夢十夜など程遠い、夢をみる暇さえなく叩き起こされた。半分は眼が覚めていない状態で聞いていた。立っていても体が揺れるような感じであった。

夜が明ける前に江画嶋は先発組の一員となり出発した。数時間後に現地到着、ただちに通信適地で指揮管理回線をつくり現地情報を迅速に伝える任務に就いた。そして救援作業本隊の進入に備えた。

自分たちの糧食や水などの生活用品と通信機電源用燃料の追加分は後段の組が持って来る

ように計画されていた。即動のために必要最小限の物で賄い、現場と司令部の通信確保を迅速、最優先にするためである。

「江画嶋、勝枝、水筒の水は満杯に入れて来たか」

「はい、満杯です」

「めし缶と乾パンは持って来たか」

「はい、最少日数分です。黒木三曹分も忘れていません」

「ありがとう、とにかく頑張ろう」

「はい」「はい」

「江画嶋は先発でよかったなー、この仕事は後の組が長期になるからな、班長の思い入れだ。通学者に気を遣って」

江画嶋は気を引き締めた。

時間の経過とともに救助作業本隊が徐々に到着して展開を開始する。それに先駆けて上村電話班が難所を有線で隈無く張り巡らした。各部隊はその有線に取り付けた野外電話機を使い出す。

黒木三曹に連絡が来た。電話機の通話音に雑音が混ざり、相手の声がよく聞き取れないということであった。

「江画嶋、勝枝、全チャンネルが悪いそうだ。今からアンテナを建て直す。中継組の山は敷地が狭く通信所移転は出来ない、という情報を小橋AM組がすばやく受信し、井上信務電信

38

組が迅速に情報解析した。こちらが送受二本とも移動させる。悪いときは、又、建て直す。

骨幹通信は責任重大だ」

「江画嶋、了解」「勝枝、了解」

三号館一階学生食堂でライスカレーを食べ、冷たい瓶牛乳の一気飲みをして喉を潤した江画嶋は図書館に来た。チョコレート色のタイルで飾られた四階建て図書館は、日が落ちて暗くなるころになると、近代的照明機器に照らされた学生閲覧室の窓中は、他の建物よりも浮かびあがる。照度も、そして彩度も増してゆく。二階入り口閲覧室は各新聞が並べられ、パンフレット、小冊子、雑誌もあり、出逢いロビーとともに集まり場所となっていた。江画嶋は新聞の一面を見て、パラパラと捲り、次の新聞に移る。地震の記事はどの新聞にも無かった。派遣は二週間で引き揚げがあり、後の組と一緒に帰って来た。取り敢えずの事後整備も終ったので、遅れるとは分かっていたが、前時限の終りごろに大学に来たのであった。来たかったのだ。文学履修の日だったからである。

参考図書閲覧室には十数人が静かに勉強していた。江画嶋はその奥の入室を図書館の勤務職員に尋ねた。丁寧に教えてもらい有り難くその中に入った。

開閉架式室で夏目漱石の作品全集類の前に立ったのだ。整然と隙間なく並び、静かに棚を独占している。江画嶋は一瞬、高価過ぎる物を見た様に思った。

江画嶋は左手首にはめている腕時計を見た。後時限の始まりにはまだ時間があった。棚を

ゆっくり眺めた。異なる柄と色の背表紙があり、全て二十数冊ずつあった。一冊引き出すことが整頓されている全集そのものに悪いような錯覚を覚えた。いままで本を見てそのようなことを意識することは無かった。この意識はすぐ別な思いを回らした。

入り口閲覧室に戻った。前時限を終えた者が数多くいてその中に交えた。二週間振りの大学生時間を感じた時だった。

３３３講義室に来た。後ろの入り口から入る時に、前から入る三、四人のグループが眼に入った。その中にあの女子学生もいた。講義室に入れば既にいつものところに着席していた女先輩と目が合った。右手を顔の所まで上げ、手の平が見えるいつもの挨拶を交わした江画嶋は、女先輩の言い付けを守り、前の方に行った。なぜか、あのとき座った席よりも二列後ろの左隅に座った。妙に座り心地が良かったが、何かに負けた思いもした。

〈挨拶をして部屋を出て、玄関正面へ来て、向うを見ると、長い廊下の果が四角に切れて、ぱっと明るく、表の緑が映る上り口に、池の女が立っている。はっと驚いた三四郎の足は、早速の歩調に狂いが出来た。その時透明な空気の画布の中に暗く描かれた女の影は一足前へ動いた。二人は人筋道の廊下の何処かで擦れ違わねばならぬ運命を以て互いに近付いて来た。〉

蒲池教授が途中「会いますよー」と解説した。

〈女はやがて・・・・・・・・・、まともに男を見た。二重瞼の切長の

「どうです、女性の描き方。これは美人、いや良い部類の方の、あれ、ですが、皆さんはど
のように描かれるでしょうね」

この日もドッときた。女性もだが、少ない男性の笑い声のほうが高かった。それも前後左右
を見ながら弾けた。江画嶋もそうだったが二列前の中のほうを見て、後ろの先輩のことも思
い、含み笑いをした。

〈女は行き過ぎた。三四郎は立ったまま、女の後姿を見守っている。・

・・・・・・途端に振り返った。三四郎は赤面するばかりに狼狽した。

・・・・・女の影は右へ切れて白い壁の中へ隠れた。〉

「ここからがこの作品の主題に入るのですが、また次に会うまでページが重なります」

〈三四郎の魂がふわつき出した。講義を聴いていると、遠方に聞

える。・・・・・その内秋は高くなる。食慾は進む。二十三の青年

が・・・・・・・・・三四郎には三つの世界が出来た。一つは

遠くにある。・・・・・・・明治十五年以前の香がする。凡てが平穏である代

りに凡てが寝坊気ている。・・・・・第二の世界のうちには・・・

太平の空気を、通天に呼吸して・・・・第三の世界は燦として春の如

く・・・そうして凡ての上の冠として美しい女性がある。・・・・・

美しい女性は沢山ある。美しい女性を翻訳すると色々になる〉

「東京と明治の時代が三四郎の言葉に表されていますが、これは漱石の代弁です。そして女性観を絡めていきますが、これは三四郎にとって日常の行動は女性への思いを土台にして進みます。どうです、沢山あるといいながら神経質ですよね」

〈・・・・庭木戸がすうと明いた。そうして思も寄らぬ池の女が庭の中にあられた。・・・・三四郎はこの狭い囲いの中に立った池の女を見るや否や、忽ち悟った。―花は必ず、剪って瓶裏に眺むべきものである―女はこの句を冒頭において会釈した。・・会釈しながら三四郎を見詰めている。〉

「さあー、これからです。というところで皆さん大変失礼ですが、今日の講義はここで終りとしたいのです。急な用事が出来て三〇分早いのですが。次の講義を楽しみにしていてください」

江画嶋はこの文学の講義を受けたいがために、遅くなっても大学に出て来た。皮肉なことに、その講義が一時間で終るのである。女先輩は定時の帰るバスに乗るから図書館に行くと言う。江画嶋は迷ったがそのままバス停に行くと言った。図書館には、つい一時間前に利用していたことも原因だった。三階から二階に降りて、二本のポール水銀灯が照らす二階通路を使って図書館二階に行き、そこから一階に降り、出逢いロビーに来た。同僚などは講義終了まであと三〇分ある。仕事の疲労を少し感じていたが、大学前のバス停の次のバス停まで歩く決心をした。一人で、本を片手に夜空を仰ぎながら歩くのも又いいだろう。掲示板に目を通し

42

て出逢いロビーを出た。並木道まで来ると、左側奥にある数棟の公務員宿舎小窓がほとんど灯っている。就寝するにはまだ早いときなのだろう。まだ営みが動いている。

男ばかりの、時間に厳しい隊内で寝泊まりする団体生活、極論的にいえば束ね縛られているような生活を送っている江画嶋にすれば、家庭生活のほのかな匂いがやさしい里を思い起こす。

並木道を出て向こうには渡らず、すぐ右に折れ、一人歩きが始まった。

夜の冷たい空気は疲れた体を解してくれる。昼間の強い慌ただしさから解放されたような穏やかな時間である。静か過ぎず、ほどほどに街の通りも照らされ、行き交う人も疎らにある。午後九時前の大学近辺だ。

最初に渡る広い交差点の信号の青が点滅し始めた。小走りに駆け抜けた江画嶋は、両側の停止線で待っていた僅かな台数の車が放つヘッドライトが、信号変わりと同時に交じり合うのを振り返り見ながら、渡り切ったところのすぐ角にある喫茶店前の歩道に来た。備え置かれた店名を記した電気機器、硝子戸の中に招く飾り灯などで、辺りよりはハッキリと明るくなっている。

途端に前を歩いている女性に気付いた。読みを教えてくれたあのあの女子学生だった。江画嶋は歩幅を少し広げ、四、五歩でその横に並ぶや否や語りかけた。

「この前はありがとう」

声を掛けられたその女子学生は立ち止まって江画嶋を見た。一瞬、気を取られた表情でそ

の声に反応はなかった。「えっ」と言うような、細かい口元の動きとともに、すぐ落ち着いた表情に戻り、江画嶋を見詰めた。

江画嶋は、また、言った。

「教えてくれてありがとう、さんしろーの、えー、文学のとき」

「あー、あれ」と一寸微笑した顔から声が返ってきた。当然、たいしたものではないような言い方だった。

だが江画嶋はお礼の気持ちが伝わったことを確認して満足感に浸った。そしてあの時のことを憶えてくれていたのを嬉しがった。

その後、もうその話はしなかった。

「いつも歩いて帰るの?」

「いいえ、早く終わったから、友だちと初めてこの通りを歩いて帰っていたのです。次のバス停までと決めて。そうしたら彼女、忘れ物をした、と大学に引き返したところです。あとは定時の大学発でそのまま帰ると言って…」

「僕も、ときには星を観ながら歩くのもいいかなーと思って」

「わーっ」

「ところで君、歩くの早いね、足、大きくなるよ」

「失礼ですね、私のいつもの歩き方です。でもこの靴、歩き難いー」

「昼はどんなところに勤めているの」

44

「病院事務です」

「家から通って?」

「いいえ、下宿を借りて、そこからです」

「そおー、僕は、これ、パーン　パーン」と言いながら銃を撃つ動作をした江画嶋は少し照れた。

「そおですか。でも全然みえませんよ。きついでしょー、訓練など」

「そんなことないよ。馴れれば」

仕事の話題から徐々に話しが弾んでいった。二人は次のバス停、次、次のバス停、そして次の、でなく、そのまま乗り換えのバス停まで歩いた。自然にそうなった。乗るべきバスが素通りしても何も思わなかった。時間にして約三〇分、それでも江画嶋には歩く距離が大分短く感じられた。

光少ない橋を渡り、左に折れながら緩やかな下り道を過ぎ、市電の始着点が見える交差点まで来ると、それまでの閑静な夜道よりも少し動きがある。だが夕方のあの賑わいに比べれば相当落着いている。夜に走るバスや市電の内部は、まわりの暗さと光増す車内灯で様子がはっきりと見える。午後九時過ぎの時間は、大体において一日の行動を終え、家路へと急いでいる人々が乗っているのだろう。立っている乗客も多くはない。

江画嶋には、普段のそんな平凡な夜景色も、今日は普通に映らなかった。目新しい、まったく違ったものになっていた。

45

駐屯地へ帰るための乗り換えバス停のすぐ傍で、相手から「ここから近いのでバスには乗らず、そのまま歩いて帰ります」と言われた江画嶋はハッとした。

その女子学生は、乗り換えバスが曲がる方向へ歩いて行った。江画嶋は思った。帰る方向は同じだったのだと。名前はなぜか聞かなかった。別れた江画嶋は十五、六メートル歩いていつもの薬園町のバス停に立った。

道路向かい側にある映画の看板は、その方向から曲がって来る車のライトに照らされていた。

江画嶋はそのなかの一つの映画題名　〝若者たち〟　を見つめた。

六

ズチャッ、ヌチャッ、ザアー、ザアー、ザアー

戦闘靴の中が雨で水浸しである。靴の外は黒い泥が厚く粘着して重たい。周辺のほとんどのところが泥濘で歩くのに苦労する。酷い場所は足がはまって抜けない。戦闘服のズボンは泥ズボンだ。雨衣を着ても何もならない、雨と汗で全身がびしょ濡れである。

悪戦苦闘を続けていると、夜明けとともに闇の暗さが薄くなってきた。辺りの形状が徐々に分かるようになってきた。だがそれと平衡するように、降る雨線も僅かに見えるようになってきた。明るくなるに従って通信所施設群の輪郭も見え出すので、隠蔽用の偽装を施しているところだ。江画嶋は合同通信所一員として昨夜からこの一帯の森へ進入、数時間を要しての通信所開設の任務に就き、通信網の構成も完了した後の仕上げの仕事である。夜通しの作業だ。

また班長の罵声が渦巻く、周囲には聞こえないように低く、強く、鋭く。

「こらー、モタモタするなー、江画嶋ー、気を抜けば、間に合わないぞー、日が昇るぞ」

「ハイ、急いで高い草を切りに奥の坂下に行きます」

「草をガサガサさせるなよー」

「了解しました」

雨も止み、徐々に完全な朝になり遠くの山並みも雲の隙間から見えて来た。朝靄も立ちこめている。一帯の移動通信シェルターやアンテナ、その他の物も何か所に埋もれているか分からなくなっている。静かな森そのままである。幾種類かの鳥の声が共鳴増幅されて響く。江画嶋の、濡れながらも動き続けて熱かった身体は、冷え切った草人形になった。通信も問題なく運用中だ。だが一夜の大仕事を遣り遂げた満足感で大自然も味方に感じてきた。薄弱い朝の光が茂みの間から射して来た。少し腰掛けよう。

気が安まったとき、急に白い文鳥のようなものがチヨ、チヨの鳴き声で、汚くなっている手に乗って来た。可愛い、いつか逢ったような、女性のような…。

「こらー、状況中だ、監視を怠るなー」の声、ハッとした。一瞬眠った、疲れた、寒い。

江画嶋は五日ぶりにバスに乗るために、葉が茂り重なり合う並木坂を下って行く。雨は降っているが、そぼ降る雨には江画嶋の気持は心和んでいた。今日も前時限には遅刻だが、同僚たちは大学に着いているところだろう。同僚とバスに乗合しないが、これはこれで良いことだろう。自分の世界に浸れる。そう思いながらの足取りである。

雨の日のバスは乗車者が多い。人の体温と濡れた傘などにより中の空気が湿り、窓の内側が曇って外が視難くなる。どのバスも同じだ。

乗り換えバス停は開いた傘の列で混雑していた。道路もゆっくり走る車で渋滞気味であ
る。市電も線路に近づく車で、チン、チン、と鳴る回数が多い。遅れる覚悟で通学している

48

江画嶋の気持は普段通りだった。乗るために、傘をつぼめた後の人々の動作は速い。濡れないように丸めた体を急いでバス中に突進させる。周りはあまり気にしない。江画嶋もそんな中で乗車した。

いつものように、出口に近い前の方の吊り輪を握りにいった。すぐ目の前の左一列席、前から三番目の座席が空いていた。普段、よほど乗客が少ないときでない限り座席には座らない江画嶋だが、今日も隣に立っている客に譲るつもりで立ったままにした。隣の客も座る様子はない。吊り輪を握っている右腕の方へ顔を動かした。隣の立人も江画嶋の方を見て会釈をした。驚いた江画嶋も瞬きした目礼で返した。微笑んだ頬が少し紅く染まっているような相手の顔を視た江画嶋も笑顔になった。曇った窓ガラスで外は見えないままである。あごを僅かに二、三回突出し、座席を勧めたので、ためらいながらも立人はうれしそうに腰を下ろした。江画嶋はあの女子学生と混んだバスで会ったのだ。

声を出して話し掛けることはしなかった。そして座っている人に、立った状態の上からは話せなかった。女子学生が江画嶋の歴史学の教科書と文庫本が入った小鞄を自分の膝の上で持ってくれたので、江画嶋は持っている物が傘だけになり、身体が非常に軽く感じた。

外の景色は閉ざされ、前席の背もたれに目線を向けたままあの女子学生は座っている。大学まで大きい交差点は二か所しかない。その間に歩道のための信号機が一か所、雨の日でバスの速度が遅いとはいっても、すぐ大学に着く。最初の交差点は青ですぐ通り過ぎた。大きいフロントガラスのワイパーは動き続けている。橋に来た。

江画嶋は吊り輪を左手に持ち替えた。右手で女子学生の肩をポンと軽く叩いてすぐ横の窓の曇りに、ナ、マ、エ、と人差し指で小さく書いていった。それを見た女子学生は少し間を置いて、やはり一指し指で、ア、イ、ウ、エ、とその横に書いた。女子学生も頷き、また中指を添えて消した。江画嶋も、エ、ガ、シ、マ、と書いた。女子学生も頷き、また微笑んだ。江画嶋も書いた名前を広く消した。その消した部分は曇りがとれ、そこだけは外の街並みが走り出した。女子学生はその窓を見続けた。

大学前に来た。立っていた乗車者から先に降りていくので二人は離れる。江画嶋は小鞄を受け取りながら聞いた。

「ありがとう、前時限はなに?」

「経済学」

聞いた江画嶋はバスから降りてそのまま三号館へ向かった。前時限が始まってまだ二〇分しか経っていなかったので、受講するためにそのまま二階の324講義室に入った。

席に着いた江画嶋は教科書を無造作に開いた後、ノートに挟んでいた授業時間割表を見た。「経済学、経済学」332講義室と記入されていた。「同じ三号館か」

前時限が終わり、三階に移動するために階段に来ると女先輩も上るところであった。

「江画嶋、久しぶり、頑張ったね、別府の山は雨で大変だったでしょう」

「今日の昼に帰って来ました」

「今日ぐらい休めば良かったのに」

「いいえ、美人先輩に会いたいので、そんなことは出来ません」

「うれしいねー」

「前時限は経営学を受けたのでしょう。325で」

「そうだよー、なんでまた、そういうことを聞くの」

「いえ、あのー」

短い一〇分間の休み時間は貴重な時間である。333講義室は語り合う仲間のグループが多い。特に女性の笑い声がいっぱいである。語ることで終日の勤務の疲れも忘れて、次の講義でも働く若人の真剣な瞳が黒板に、ノートに集注する。

「美人先輩、ここはいつも派手やかで、明々としていますね」

「君たち男性もいろいろな事を話し合いなさい、恋の話など」

「ギャホー」

「冗談、冗談、早く前に行きなさい」

追いやられて、江画嶋自ら思った消極的な、前回座った席に着いた。

〈三四郎は自分の今の生活が熊本当時のそれよりも、ずっと意味の深いものになりつつあると感じた。曾て考えた三個の世界のうちで、第二第三の世界は正にこの・・・・・〉

教授は今日も読み人を指名して言った。

「面白くなりましたねー、大賑わいの菊人形展を見に行った三四郎はどうなったでしょう。

51

この小説の最大のところです。ここは女性に読んでもらいましょう」

江画嶋は曇りガラス窓の名前のことを思い出した。ア、イ、ウ、エ、を授業時間割表にメ

モしていた。どういう漢字なのか、当然、苗字だろう。

〈・・・美禰子は又向こうをむいた。見物に押されて、さっさと出口

の方へ行く。三四郎は群衆を押し分けながら、・・・・・・。女は人込

の中を・・・。三四郎も無論一所に歩き出した。半町ばかり来た時、

女は人の中で留まった。

「此処は何処でしょう」

三四郎は・・・

「もう一町ばかり歩けますか」と美禰子に聞いてみた。

「歩きます」

二人はすぐ石橋を渡って・・・・・・・・・しばらく河の緑を上がると、もう

人は通らない。

広い野である。女は・・・・・。

「美しい事」と云いながら、草の上に腰を卸した。

三四郎も・・草の上に坐った。

・・・・・・・・・・・・・

「もう気分は宜くなりましたか。宜くなったら、そろそろ帰りましょ

52

うか」

「迷子」

女は三四郎を見たままでこの一言を繰返した。三四郎は答えなかった。

「迷子の英訳を知っていらしって」

三四郎は知るとも、知らぬとも・・・・・・

「教えて上げましょうか」

「ええ」

「迷える子　解かって？」

迷える子という言葉は解かった様でもある。又解からないようでもある。・・・・・・すると女は急に真面目になった。

「私そんなに生意気にみえますか」

三四郎は美禰子の態度を故の様な・・・・・・・・・女は辛然として

・・・「じゃ、もう帰りましょうか」と云った。・・・・・・

・・・二人はその見当へ歩いて行った。・・・・・・・

・・・三四郎が何か云おうとすると、足の前に泥濘があった。・・・

・・・その真中に足掛りの為に手頃な石を置いたものがある。三四郎

は石の扶を藉らずに、すぐ向うへ飛んだ。そうして美禰子を振り返っ

て見た。　美禰子は右の足を泥濘の真中にある石の上へ乗せた。

53

・・・・・・・・三四郎は此方側から手を出した。

「御捕まりなさい」

「いえ大丈夫」と女は笑っている。手を出している間は、調子を取るだけで渡らない。三四郎は手を引込めた。すると美禰子は石の上にある右の足に身体の重みを託して、左の足でひらりと此方側へ渡った。あまりに下駄を汚すまいと念を入れ過ぎた為め、力が余って、腰が浮いた。のめりそうに胸が前へ出る。その勢いで美禰子の両手が三四郎の両腕の上へ落ちた。

「迷える子」と美禰子が口の内で云った。三四郎はその呼吸を感じる事が出来た。〉

「きれいな声でありがとう。何ページ読んでもらったか忘れましたね―。みんなうっとりして、漱石もうれしいことでしょう。迷える子、ここにいる女性諸君のことでしょうかそれとも男性…」

周りの女性群の小さな笑い声が江画嶋に響いた。

「次は運動会の日の池端でのちょっとした絡みがありますが、それまでは、学生集会での熊本の赤酒、また馬肉、そして野蛮な熊本などを語りながら進みます。漱石が赤酒を飲んだなんて、親しみを感じますね。明治の学生気質、これもおもしろいですね。色々なタイプの理想追い。学生の時の漱石はどうだったのでしょうか」

江画嶋は教授の話を聞きながら、また、ア、イ、ウ、エ、を考えた。ア、イ、コ、イ、ま

さかそういうことはなかろう。漢字にしたら、愛、恋、になる。

〈三四郎は・・・・・自分は田舎から出て大学へ這入ったばかりである。

学問という学問もなければ見識と云う見識もない。自分が・・・尊敬

を美禰子から受け得ないのは・・・・・。そう云えば何だか、あの女

に・・・・・いる様である。〉

「漱石も恋をしたのですかね。三四郎は田舎者で初心だから都会と女性に遅れを憶えて行き

ますが、漱石は逆に、東京人だったから、そのようなことはなかったでしょう。ここは門下

生がモデルだといわれていますが」

東京が都会で熊本が田舎なら、生まれ育った自分の里の町は何だろう。そこから来て今は

熊本にいる。江画嶋は考えた。熊本は都会だ、田舎町から出て来た自分も、この物語の主人

公と同じである。だがこの主人公とは違い、レベルの低い自分である。自分が物語の主人公

になればレベルの低い物語になるだろう。

熊本という街の中にいるだけでいいのだ。

この小説を知っただけで良かったのだ。

授業終了、今日に限って、考えなくてもいい事を考えた江画嶋は、後方で語らっている女

先輩の明るい姿を見て、その考えたことを忘れた。不思議なものだった。

「美人先輩、バス停まで一緒に語りながら帰りましょう」

「いいよ、なにを今更」

「今日は美人先輩の文学論を聞きたいです」

「ハハーン、印象が強かったのね、いまの講義。文学は理性と情緒の争いから生まれるの、理論的にいかないのよ」

「暖かい夢、夢物語ですかね、小説は」

「江画嶋、普通に、普通に、江画嶋は普通だから」

先輩の言う事が妙におもしろかった。帰る時間には雨は降っていなかった。一霎模様である。大山が、畳んだこうもり傘を大きく振りながら追っかけて来た。

「大先輩、江画嶋先輩、霧のロンドン、いや霧の大江町ですね」

「江画嶋、漱石流に俳句を作らない」

「美人先輩、漱石と俳句のときの講義は欠席しましたので分かりません」

「なあーに、五、七、五、で作ればいいの。こんなのどお？　夜の霧ロンドン風の街路灯。名句でしょう」

「さすがー、僕も一句。変化して霧の大学ロンドンか。いいでしょう」

「二人の先輩、文学を習っていない僕が一句。漱石を語るふたりは霧まみれ。上手でしょう」

「三人、霧ばかりね。霧か霞か靄か解からないよ、それに季語になるのかなー、まあ、いいや、後輩と三人寄れば俳句知恵」

「漱石もいいですがいつか飲みに行きましょう。雨時は暇なんです、大工は」

56

「暇、私たちは日曜日だけよ遊びに行けるのは、そうでしょう江画嶋」

「美人先輩、日曜日は外出できません。居残りです」

「そうか、待機の日か。江画嶋も厳しいね…。よし、明日土曜日の後時限は二人とも休講だったね。私、サボるから遊びに行きましょう」

霞んだ灯の並木道途中で話はまとまった。正門付近そこだけが、霞の中の丸いトンネル出口のようになって先の道路をはっきり見せていた。

七

　ドス、ドドー、ドス、ドドー、ドス、ドドー

　基本動作が終わり、体が解れたが蒸し暑さも手伝ってもう汗が流れて来た。

「面、着けー」

　面をかぶっただけで息苦しさを感じた。

「第二教習、始め！」

　応用動作でもう息があがった。

「まわれ！」

　相手が替わる。習い始めの松下二士など部下たちは長身ばかり。

「初一本、始め！」

　小走りで体当たり突き合うが、左腕ばかり突かれ痺れる。

「気合と迫力が無い、当たりが弱い、もう一度、始め！」

　相手の木銃の先があごに入り、激痛が走る。

「全員、声が低い、もう一度、突けぇ！」

　回数が増えるに従い気持と体が高揚して、中野教官の大声が気持よく聞こえてきた。シャッと道衣は汗でビッショリである。調子が出て来た。

58

「やめー、面をとって休憩、防具は肩だけとっていい、だが休憩が終わったらすぐ試合だぞ」

江画嶋は面と籠手をとり、肩防と胴を身体から外した。外の空気の美味しさが身に沁みる。

武道場から外に出ると、外の空気の美味しさが身に沁みる。この時の体の軽さは凄い。そして

「こらー、誰が胴をとっていいと言った。休憩やめー、すぐ準備して集合ー、負け残り試合を始める。　最後まで残ったものは大特訓だー」

江画嶋は他の大勢の者が強く見え出した。とっさの判断が明暗を分ける武道の試合は一刻の猶予もままならない。

「突け」「突けー」「突けぇー」

小庭に映る蘇鉄の影は、側にある一号館、四号館の学び人を照らす灯りが創り出し、芝の緑は対照的に浮き出て鮮やかである。一千二百名が学ぶ二部の講義時間の学園は、昼間の学園とは違った趣を醸し出す。

江画嶋と大山は前時限が五分ほど早く終わり、二人で先輩を待つことにした。

休講の者は次々と出逢いロビーを通り抜けて行った。

「大先輩はほんとうに後時限をサボるのでしょうか」

「大山、美人先輩は、嘘はつかないさ、顔はああでも心は美人だから。おれが美人先輩と言っているのはそういうことだよ」

「江画嶋先輩、楽しみですね、三人で飲みに行けるなんて」

二人が話し出してすぐ女先輩がいつもの挨拶動作で現れた。大山は安心した表情で「無理しなくていいですよ」と言ったがその声は小さかった。

正門前で先輩は通りかかったタクシーを拾った。繁華街の通町筋に来た。タクシーから降りた三人は下通り商店街を歩き出した。土曜日の夜は賑わっていて、学びの場所から一気に来たことで、江画嶋と大山は頭のサイクルが一瞬切り替らなかった。眼も定まらない。通常にない華やかさに見えた。先輩が行くままに付いて行った。この一番街通りには屋根が覆い被されていて新天街と名付けされている。将来は通り全部が上通りと同様にアーケード街として歩行者専用道路になると先輩は二人に説明していった。

「ここだよ」

きれいな小料理屋に入った。畳席の長方形の台を挟み江画嶋と大山が並んで座り、その二人の先輩が向かいに一人で座った。店の女将さんと雑談した女先輩は二人に希望料理を聞くこととはせず、すぐビールを持って来させた。

「君たち、何時までいいの」

「大山は」

「土曜日の消灯だけは一時間遅れの十一時で、その一〇分前まで帰隊、あ、帰らなけ…」

「国鉄の最終は、えーと」

「いま八時半だから、十時まではいいでしょう。二人とも」

「はい」江画嶋と大山は二人揃って返事した。

「じゃー乾杯、この店の名前は、しぐれ。店長は私の知り合い。郷土料理セットを頼んでいるから美味しいものがいっぱい来るよ、いっぱい食べなさい、先ずは馬刺しから」

江画嶋は武道訓練で疲れていたので大変有り難かった。

「美人先輩、今日は仕事に勉強に遊びに、ボリュウムたっぷりの一日です。大山、そうだろう」

「江画嶋先輩、僕もです。今日は雨が降らなかったから外の仕事が十分に捗って、いい疲労感が残っていてこの料理、牛鍋は最高に旨く、体に栄養満点ですね」

二人の満足な表情に、女先輩も喜んだ。聴き慣れたBGMが程良い音量で流れている。

「この曲いいね、『シバの女王』レイモン・ルフェーブル、さっきのも良かったでしょー、『青春の光と影』誰が歌っているか知っている、江画嶋？」

「ジュディー・コリンズですよ」

「正解、じゃー『悲しき天使』は」

「メリー・ホプキンス」

「この頃いい新曲ばかり。あれもきれいな曲だったねー、去年の『白い恋人たち』フランシス・レイの」

「クロード・ルルーシュの映画、グルノーブル冬のオリンピックのテーマ曲ですね」

「少し前ではブラウンズの『谷間に三つの鐘が鳴る』もきれいな曲だった。それとビリー・ボーン楽団の『真珠貝の歌』『峠の幌馬車』、パーシー・フェイス管弦楽団の『夏の日の

「夏の日の恋は夜のラジオ番組、〈こんばんは五條です〉のテーマ曲として思い出します」

「喫茶店のサテライトスタジオからの放送、江画嶋も聴いていたのか。大山は」

「ぼくはあまり…」

「そうなの…、浪曲でしょう聴いていたのは」

「そんなに古い人間ではありません」

「ごめんね、それとブラザース・フォア、キングストン・トリオ、ジョーン・バエズなどのフォークソングも好きだよ。江画嶋はミッチー・ミラーも好きでしょう、『クワイ河マーチ』『史上最大の作戦マーチ』勇ましい曲だから。だけど、〈ミッチと歌おう〉のテレビ番組ではいろんな曲を歌っていたよね」

「美人先輩もほんとうに色々知っていますね。感心します」

「映画はどぉー」

「映画も好きですよ。特に高校三年の秋に七十ミリで観た『サウンド・オブ・ミュージック』良かったですね。わざわざ熊本に急行バスで観に来ました。お客さんが多かったので座ることが出来ず立って観ました。画面の綺麗さで、ざわめきが起きていました」

「私も勿論観たわ、でもやはり『ウエスト・サイド物語』歌にも踊りも感動したよ」

「西部劇も好いでしょう。小さい頃と高校の時のリバイバルで観たジョン・フォード監督の『黄色いリボン』モニュメントバレーの夕陽は名場面です。音楽も最高です」

恋」などは最高」

「リボンが黄色、この意味知っている？　江画嶋」

「もちろんです。あれって、あの意思表示のしるしです」

「そうーあれよ。ところで私たち西洋かぶれ、特にアメリカかぶれをしているね、しかたがないか、戦後貧乏だった日本、その中で小さい頃からアメリカの豊かで明るい生活を見せ付けられれば…。大山はどんなのが好き」

「僕は日本の歌謡曲です。『ブルーライト横浜』のような」

「いしだあゆみ、君たちと同じぐらいだろう、年齢」

「江画嶋先輩と同じです」

「大山は二つ下か、君たちは多かったよねー、ベビーブームの三学年」

「江画嶋先輩がその第一陣です。二十二年、二十三年生まれが」

「そのままで行けば今の四年生ね。同じ歳でどれくらいが大学生になっていると思う、大学と短大合わせて十六か十七パーセント。新聞の資料で見たよ。下の学年は僅かに増えているけどそんなに変わらない。　優秀な人だけだよ」

「僕たち二部はその数の中に入っているのですか」

「どうかな、入ってないでしょう。でも大学で勉強するだけでも幸せと思いなさい」

周りの客の二、三組が入れ替わった。飲むビールの本数は少なかったが、先輩の顔は赤くなってきた。途中、話の内容が急に展開した。

「文学の話でいこう。さあー注いで、注いで、文学で心に栄養を」

声が一段大きくなり、続いた。

「あのね、草枕、高校生のとき読んだの。君たちも行ったことがあるでしょう小天、蜜柑山よ。あそこが舞台になっているの。知に働けば角が立つ、情に掉させば流される、意地を通せば窮屈だ。この文句知っているでしょう。君たち」

大山は首をひねりながら言った。

「く、さ、ま、く、ら、江画嶋先輩、草をまとめた、枕のことですか」と。これに対して江画嶋は大笑いしながら「大山、教えてやろう。漱石、夏目漱石の小説の題だよ。知に働けば、は、そのはじめの部分」と得意そうに話した江画嶋に「さすが、文学を教わっている江画嶋、大山より偉いよ」と冗談交じりの女先輩、「エライかなー江画嶋先輩は」と大山は不満そうにしてビールをグイと飲んだ。

また話が動いた。

「君たち、私のこと嫌いでしょう。お説教がましくて」と言いながら今度は声の調子が普通になった。

伯父が開業している司法書士事務所を手伝っていて、大学の講義と仕事との関連を深くひしひしと感じ大変有意義であると言い出した。そのような話も、江画嶋と大山は聞き入るばかりであった。

途中で再度、話の内容が急展開した。

「この頃、大学紛争が多いでしょう、高校時代に精一杯努力して大学に入り、こんなこと

64

を。もったいないねー、親は嘆いているでしょう。何が不満なんだろう。社会は生きていくために不条理はいっぱいだよ。理想通りにはいかないの。それが常だよ。組織の中の正義と真の正義も又違うような気がするけど……。それに迷惑かけちゃーいけないよ、投石をしたり、角棒を振ったりは。勇気があるならタオルで顔を隠さないことね、弱虫のやることだよ。他の学生はまじめに授業を受けているのに。私の個人主義かなー。だけど優秀な学生には理想と正義をどんどん追求して行ってもらいたいよ」

「そうですね」と二人は顔を見合わせた。

「真の正義の味方はここにいる。君たち」

「はー、はい」

「江画嶋、時々は家に帰っているかな」

「いいえ、赤酒を飲んだ正月以来帰っていません」

「だめだよー、帰ってあげなさい。顔を見せるだけで親は喜ぶんだから、それが孝行というものだよ。手紙を出すような遠いところでもないし、近いからさー」

「はい」

「だけど、親になって見なければ親の気持ちは解からないとよく言うわねー……。若い時の良さも年寄りなってみなければ解からないとも言うし」

台の上いっぱいに並べられた大皿、小皿の取り物も少量になっていた。男性二人は満腹も満腹になり、頭の中もそのようになった。勘定は女性ひとりが引き受けた。

三人は、まだ賑やかそのままの通町筋で別れ、一人は親戚の住み込み先に、一人は就寝ラッパが鳴る建物へ、一人は鋸、鉋が並ぶ自宅へ、と帰って行った。

66

八

「掘り終ったかー」

　ガッザッ、バァザッ、バァザッ

「通信所掩体完了でーす」

「よーし、終ったところから点検する。不備なところがある班は休憩なしで修正せよ」

　梅雨明けの日差しは容赦なく照りつける。杭夫、ん、ん、高風な青年達の完全装備を身につけた掩体構築訓練はそのなかで行われ、ようやく終わった。乾ききっていない演習場の土と格闘した身体は、下から上がる湿気との戦いでもあった。前日までと打って変わった急な高温も厳しかった。

「訓練には最適な日だ。穴掘り後は今日も駆け足で帰隊する。各班、隊伍を崩さぬように走れ。だが体の調子が悪いものは言い出せ。エンピ、ツルハシは確実に車載せよ」

「車両に搭乗する者なし、全員走ります」

「よし、スピードは要求しない。完走が目標だ。気分が悪くなった者は遠慮なく歩いてもよし。だが若いから頑張れると思う」

　江画嶋は走り切った。到着解散後は我先にと洗面所に走り、水道蛇口をひねった。地下水だけの水の冷たさと旨さに、涙が湧き出た。

「こらー、ゴックン、ゴックン、ゴックン、アー、アー
び集合、集合ー」
「こらー、水は出しっぱなしにするなー、今から泥で汚れた床の清掃を実施する。全員、再

開いた窓の外から夜風が流れてきて気持ち良い。文学講義室で初めて窓側の席に座った江
画嶋は半分満足だった。夏のはじめ、この時期の学生の服装もすっかり替わった。勤務場所
からそのままのネクタイ姿の通学者も、暑くなればネクタイをはずした白の半袖姿のまま
だ。講義科目により履修者の多い講義室は当然に暑くなる。文学が行われる講義室は満席に
近いのでそうなるところだが、読まされる緊張感からか、講義の面白さからか、暑さなどは
全く感じさせない雰囲気だ。
「美禰子が言った、迷える子、のところから数回になりますが、よく三四郎は神経を使いま
すね。この世は男もう、女もうようよ、若者うようよ、悩まなくてもいいのにと、皆
さんお思いになりません。だけど、ここがいいのでしょうね、小説は」
〈夕暮れには、まだ間があった。・・・・・美禰子と一所に表へ出た。
・・・こう云う機会を、随意に造る事は、三四郎に取って困難である。
三四郎は長く引延ばして・・・・・。並んで歩きながら、・・・・・〉
「この章の、この後の展開から、ああ、私は皆さんに読ませたくありません。ああ」
教授の大袈裟な演技に学生たちは大笑いになった。この小説を既に読み終わっている者も

講義に沿って読んでいるものにとっても重要展開部分であった。江画嶋も楽しくなって笑いながらずっと後の席を何気なく見た。同じように笑っている女先輩を見て何か安心した気持になった。女先輩は江画嶋が見ているので江画嶋に小さく手を振った。江画嶋も遠慮なく手を振った。

江画嶋にしてみれば、毎回этого文学の講義九〇分間は真剣で静かなときと、笑いで賑やかなときの静と動の組み合わせで瞬く間に終了する感じである。

この講義室にいる一人一人と、学んでいる時と時間を共用している。同じ時代の中で生きている。そんな感傷も抱いた。

九

タッ、タッ、タッ、タッ

日曜日の休日に警衛勤務に就いている江画嶋は午後の当番時間の見廻り後、本哨に戻った。

控え時間に入ろうとしたとき警衛司令から勤務命令が下った。

「江画嶋士長、面会者が四名来られている。司令部前の花壇地域までお供してきなさい。見学を終えられたら、また一緒に帰って来なさい。特別命令だ」

江画嶋は緊張しながら返事した。

「はい、了解しました」と答えたが警衛司令の含み笑いの顔に戸惑った。

「江画嶋にピッタリの任務だ。天気も良い、静かな駐屯地だ。相手も喜ばれるだろう」

四名とは幼い子供三人と母親と見られる中年の女性だった。江画嶋は節度を失わない程度で案内した。四人はうれしさを隠しきれず楽しんでいた。「つつじの花が満開の時は大変きれいでしょう」と言われた江画嶋は丁寧に「ええそうです」と答えた。

その女性は続けて話した。

十八歳のときに好きな人が警察予備隊発足と同時に入隊のため、故郷を離れて行った。好きな人を奪われたようで、予備隊を憎んだ。でも私はその後、見合い結婚をして、子供が三人こんなに大きくなった。今

ずっと待っていたが、それ以来その人は帰って来なかった。

70

は幸せである。だが妙なもので駐屯地に一回だけでも入ってみたかった。こんなきれいな駐屯地を見学させてもらっていると、あの頃が想い出されて複雑でしかたがない。

江画嶋はその話を聞いて背筋を伸ばし直し、そして自分を下げないように特に親切に対応した。帰りに「今日は良い日でした」と言われた江画嶋は逆にうれしかった。

永日小品、わずかな時間に思いがけない重大な仕事をしたような、江画嶋はそんな満足感と余韻が次の日の勤務交代まで残った。

〈三四郎が何時まで立っても、恐れ云った様に控えているので先生は又話始めた。「・・・・・もっと面白い話をしよう」

「ええ」

「面白い夢を見た。・・・僕が生涯にたった一遍逢った女に、突然夢の中で再会した・・・・・・・・・」

「善くその女と云うことがわかりましたね」

「夢だよ。夢だから分かるさ。そうして夢だから不思議で好い。・・・・・僕がその女に・・・・・あなたはどうして、そう変わらずにいるのかと聞くと、この顔の年、この服装の月、この髪の日が一番好きだから・・・あなたに御目にかかった時・・・・・・。その時僕が女に、あなたは画だと云うと、女が僕に、あなたは詩だといった」

「それからどうしました」と三四郎が聞いた。

「本当の事実なんだから面白い」〉

「この小説の最終章が近づいてきました。ここからは顔に自信がない男性諸君は次のページから本を破ってください。女性諸君は自分に自信がある人、たとえば美人だとか」

ドドドッと来た。

一つの作品を軸としながら、それにまつわる文学ばなしなど教授の話術に乗せられ、漱石の文章に戸惑いながらも親しみ、また明治の時代をも十分に学ぶことができた前期の講義が終ろうとしている。夏季休講が近づいてきた。

「三四郎はここまでで後期はその他の作品に浸りましょう」

消極的な、列、の一番窓側にいた江画嶋はとうとう前期を通じて、座る席の大体の定位置を決めず、その日の気分で座って来た。読まされたあの日の席にその後行かなかった。日が進むにつれて好む席位置は大概固まってくるものであるが、文学の時だけは妙なもので気を使ってきた。こんなことを考える自分を不思議に思った。この文学の時だけのことだったが。

講義終了後、席を立ってすり足で中の通路へ向かうと、すでに通路にいたあの女子学生が江画嶋の方を見て笑みを浮かべ、軽く会釈をした。江画嶋も頭を少しだけ下げた。彼女は他の学生と喋りながら講義室を出た。

今日の江画嶋は女先輩が欠席していたことが心残りであった。十月の後期授業に触れたときだ。昔のことを喋っ

の女先輩のある一言が忘れられなかった。付き合ってくれた下通りで

ても先の事を語ることは滅多になかったのだが。

女先輩が何時も座る一番後ろの席を寂しく見ながら３３３講義室を出た江画嶋は、帰りの時間にしては珍しく図書館に来た。新聞閲覧室を覗いただけで階段を下り、出逢いロビーを見渡して通り抜けた。同僚二人にも、大山にも会う事は無かった。

江画嶋は大学へ通わなかった夏季休講が一か月半もありながら、僅かに残っている『三四郎』のページはなぜか読まなかった。そのままにして漱石の初期の作品を読むことにした。寝起きを共にしている上級者や部下に冷やかされながらも『吾輩は猫である』『坊っちゃん』を本格的に真面目に読んだ。面白く痛快だった。

大学の講義でも説明を受けていた『坊っちゃん』に登場する漱石の母なる女性の名前〝清〟に関心が出た。江画嶋の母の名前と同じだったからだ。とおり名は〝清子〟といっている。その〝清子〟は『明暗』にも使われている。『吾輩は猫である』に出てくる吾妻橋の袂のこともその母がよく話していたのを思い出した。そこは先祖が仕えた細川家支藩の下屋敷があったとよく聞いていた。

その他の作品は読まなかった。手を付けなかった。付け切れなかったのが本当だったろう。後期授業に楽しみを取って置こうと思うことも少しはあった。漱石の本を読むことで、今まで本を読んでこなかった気後れを取り戻せるような、思考力が養われるような、そんな気分にもなってきた。本屋ではあらゆる種類の新刊本に対する求知心も生じ、棚を眺めるようになった。

江画嶋のこの夏には二つの興味深い出来事があった。

一つは阿蘇で行われた九州農村青年祭である。これは沖縄も含む九州で農業を営む若者が集まり、研修と親睦を深める大きな大会で、二泊三日の日程を通して各町の青年団の応援参加もあり、『明日へのビジョンをかかげて良い町、美しい村づくりに頑張ろう』のスローガンを掲げる言わば若者の祭典である。参加者一千百名の平均年齢は二十二歳であった。江画嶋はこの大会に宿泊テント設営支援の一員で行った。支援の名目であったが、同じ若者として堂々と参加した想いだった。大草原の中で行われた最初の夜のボンファイヤー、二日目の夜の大キャンプファイヤーでは、農業従事者と青年団の心意気と元気に圧倒された。そして大学で机を並べている数人の仲間と顔を合わせたとき、江画嶋はうれしくなり仲間達との話が弾んだ。一人は「我々の同世代は数が多い。誇りを持って農業に汗を流す同世代も多いので勇気が出た」、もう一人は「大学で学ぶ農業人も知った。将来は農業文化知識人で農業は夢と希望のある仕事になる」、さらにもう一人は「村には新しい文化が花開くだろう。村から小説家を」、青年団協議会の者は「町には斬新な商店街が無数に現れることだろう。一つの店が、新しい知恵で価値ある商品をお客さんの為に揃える」、そして「その代価を将来の子供や孫など次の世代に引き継ぐ」、「要は、無計画で使い込まないことだ」など尽きなかった。

もう一つがアポロ十一号の月着陸のニュースである。人間の可能性の追求と夢に向かっての挑戦である。高校二年生の時に行なわれた東京オリンピックに興奮したが、この月着陸に

も大いに興奮した。電波伝搬の技術、通信技術、電子計算機の技術、話題は自らの仕事に直結するものばかりであり、将来の夢へ気分は盛り上がった。世界は動いている。自分も動こう。気持の高まりが続く日々の二十一歳の夏であった。

そして大学の授業開始の日が待ち遠しかった。

その頃、江画嶋は夢を見た。

教室に座っている。窓際に座っている。窓は一面のガラス張りである。桟も無い。まして壁などは無い。全てガラスだ。足元から天井まで、教室の前端から後端までガラスで出来ている。他の教室も同じだ。その教室が大きな円形となって繋がっている。互いの教室からはすべての教室が望める。幾つの教室があるのだろうか？私は数えない。どの教室も満員で真剣に講義を受けている。

中の大きな庭には緑がいっぱいである。陽光がきらめいている。木陰のベンチは学生たちの休み時間を待っているかのように構えている。細い小川もゆっくり流れている。水面には木々が映る。草や花が風に揺れる。空には雲が流れる。

光輝いていた景色が夕陽と共に夜色になった。講義はずーと続いている。教授の話は面白くて尽きない。

庭におとなしく立っていた灯火搭が点る。夜の庭は一段と教室からの眺めを楽しませ、ころを和ませる。今度は小川の流れに星と月が映える。

真向いになる遠い教室を見た。

一人がこちらを見ている。

私も見続けた。見続けた。見続けた。

秋の大学通学は前期試験から始まった。江画嶋は文学の試験はまったく出来なかった。その他の科目は上手くいったようだったが、なんと一番の不出来は文学であった。原因は文章に対する理解力の無さだった。それと回答での漢字の誤記入も多かったようだ。基礎的な国語力の欠如を思い知った。

成績表が次々と出逢いロビーに貼られていった。一連番号は男女区別のない五十音順で並び、名前、出身高が印刷されている学籍番号表の定型用紙が使用され、そこに科目履修者の点数が記入されていた。人の名前を知っていれば、その人の点数が分かる厳しいものだった。良心を責めながらも、ア、イ、ウ、エ、を探した。愛上があった。

十

銀杏の葉が黄色に色づき、その落ち葉が並木道を埋め始めていた。黄色のじゅうたんとまではいかないが、歩くときはその葉を踏まなければ歩けなかった。

深まりの秋、各科目の内容も大筋に差しかかってきた。語学や史学など教養科目も多いなか、経済学、法律学などの専門基礎などは、女先輩が言っていた仕事に直結する学生も多かった。県庁や市役所など公的な機関に勤務する者など余程そのようだ。

一号館の１２１講義室にいくため階段を上りかけた江画嶋は、一階廊下にいた女先輩を見た。声を掛けたかったが、講義開始時間が迫っていたのでそのまま階段を上って行った。女先輩が教務課の前に立っていたことを気にした江画嶋ではあったが、そのまま講義を受けた。この日の後時限は四号館の授業になっていた日であった。だが、その出逢いロビーに走って行った。交叉し語り合う学生の中に、図らずも女先輩が椅子に座っていた。手には単行本が握られていた。江画嶋を見た女先輩は非常にうれしそうな顔をした。

「この本買った？」
「草、枕、まだですよ」
話が急に変わった。

「大山はまだ来ないね。何を履修しているのかなー」

「分かりません」

「いい、聞いて、江画嶋……。辞めるの、大学を。今月、結婚するから」

「冗談でしょう。その冗談はひどいですよ」

先輩は真剣に話し出した。勤務している事務所の先輩と結婚すると言う。伯父の勧めもあったと言う。跡継ぎが無く、二人に任せたいとの事であった。

江画嶋は衝撃を受けた。女先輩との楽しかった日々の思いが駆け巡った。

「美人先輩はやっぱり心は美人だから見初められたのですね。僕もうれしいです」

「こら、江画嶋、フェイスもでしょう」

「は、はい」

「後時限はどこ」

「423です」

「もう帰るから四号館まで一緒に行こう」

二人は四号館の前に来た。道を挟み一本だけの銀杏の木が立っている。その小振りな木は、大学にある全ての電灯に照らされているかのように、夜の景色内一に輝いていた。落ち着き、淑やかな深みのある木に見えた。

「この本、あげるね。草枕、蒲池先生から習うけど、しっかり読みなさい。最後に川と駅が出て来るけど、繁根木川だと思うよ。錦川とも言っていたけど。川幅もちょうど同じ位だ

し、町中に入れば土手に柳もあるし、居酒屋さんも木材所もあるよ。舟から降りるところを錦橋の袂とすれば、まっすぐ駅まで行けるよ。だからその駅は漱石が汽車に乗るときに何時も通過していた高瀬駅と思うの。駅舎の反対側の方は、葦が生い茂り、田んぼ、が広がっていたよ。だから漱石は、葦、田、葦田、吉田の停車場、としたのよ。そして金峰山の向こうの駅ではないことは確かよ。主人公の画工は金峰山を越えて来ているのだから。まあ、私の素人考えで、ひいき目。そんなこと考えながら読めばおもしろいよ」

「はい」

「江画嶋、それから大学は四年間通しなさい、二年間ぐらいではだめだよ。仕事の都合もあるけど頑張りなさい。一生涯学び続けることが理想だけどね。学問を積んでいればいざと言う時に正しい判断が出来ると思うの。例え大きな変化が迫ってきても間違った方向に行かないためにさあー。君は信用しているよ。ごめんね、最後まで偉そうに言って。いつでもいいから遊びに来なさい」

「はい」

江画嶋は女先輩とそこで別れた。女先輩は歩きながら振り返り、いつもの右手を上げる動作をして正門に向かって行った。

呆然として立ち尽くした江画嶋だったが、すぐ貰った本を握り締め急いで四号館の階段を駆け上がり、第一外国語英語の授業開始に備えた。

後期の文学では、漱石文学の世界、と題して主要作品の梗概と鑑賞に重きが置かれていっ

た。『それから』『門』『こころ』『二百十日』など学生自身の朗読はなかったので講義の進み方が早く感じられた。だが『草枕』では『三四郎』のときのような読みながらの講義形態に戻った。秋から始まる『三四郎』の物語を春に読み、春の小説『草枕』を秋に読む、これも印象深かった。

　江画嶋は座る定位置の席を女先輩が座っていた席に決めた。隣の席は二歳年上の男になり、女先輩の噂ばなしは日が経つに連れて無くなっていった。

　その男学生は靴屋に勤めていると言い、飲食街で働いている女性の靴の修理が忙しい、新しい靴を買うことが出来ない人が多い、など厳しい生活の話を聞かせてくれる。

　あの女子学生とは、お互い挨拶は欠かさなかった。学期末試験前にはノートの貸し借りを数回行った。だが、その学期末試験で文学の単位は取れなかった。五十九点であった。あと一点を、新名、松尾の同僚二人も、大山も驚き同情した。

十一

江画嶋はあと一点の意地で次の年も文学を履修した。そして多くの漱石作品をむさぶり読んだ。お盆休暇などで帰省した数日間の里の家でも、驚く様子の家族の前で、読みまくった。

おとなしく柔らかな上品に満ちた気分に浸れる時間、文学の世界にはこれらを探し当てた。その対になる仕事は余計に頑張れるようになった。

その二年目の夏が過ぎて九月になった。最初の土曜日の夜に市民会館で行われた吹奏楽の演奏会にあの女子学生を招待した。江画嶋は次の日に日記を付けた。

"ありがとう僕のわがままを素直に受け入れてくれて、最高に素晴らしい演奏会でした。君にしてみればそうでもなかったとしても、僕にとっては忘れようとしても忘れられない夕べでした。帰りは市民会館から新天街、上通り、そしてバス停、僕はわざと一番遠いバス停を選びました。いつも遠く感じるバス停が、なぜか近くに感じました。足が痛かったでしょう。でも笑顔で僕に話題を提供してくれて、ますます君は僕の関心の人になりました。制服姿で君と短い時をすごしたことは生涯の思い出です。ありがとう"

十月の上旬、仕事で鹿児島の山に登った。長期の中継所勤務である江画嶋は、その間大学に通えなかった。同僚がいる駐屯地へ隠語の連絡をした。電送文を、あの女子学生に渡してもらうことを考えた。

〜鹿児島にある標高千百メートル山頂中継所より〜

雲につつまれ秋のかおりの中での仕事は幸福でいっぱいです。熊本の金峰山の頂上にも似たこの山は、ピクニックの人々で若々しい雰囲気です。みんな汗ビッショリになって登って来ます。みんな、こんにちは、と言ってくれて、たいへん楽しい生活です。でも二十四日までという長い期間なので、君に欠席の連絡と合わせて、僕たちの無線による楽しい通信をお送りします。

江画嶋はその二十四日土曜日の夜遅く、山から帰った。明くる日に行なわれた第二部の体育祭には参加した。珍しく昼間に集う夜間大学生は、真上から柔らかに照らす秋の陽と、突き抜けるような青い空の下で、仲良くはしゃぎ回り楽しんでいた。そして江画嶋は久しぶりにあの女子学生と挨拶を交わした。

その後キャンパスは、木々の葉も落ちて冬の佇まいを見せ始めた。十二月に入り寒さも増してきた夜間だが、教室は完備されたスチームで暖かな安らぎのなかで学習が行われていた。前時限開始十分前に324講義室に入った江画嶋は席に座った。外国史の教科書を開いた時、あの女子学生が友だちと話しながら江画嶋のすぐ前の前の席に座った。前は空席になっ

ていたので後ろ姿は近かった。その女子学生はすぐ髪を結んだ。黄色いリボンで結ばれた。

江画嶋はノートの隅に書き残した。

　"青春の日の郷愁、それは青春の日々からは遠い月の風を見るが如く、知る、ということは不可能である。だからそれを知らぬという現在に、素晴らしい毎日があると思う。しかし、それが今日に終わることのないように、明日への宿題を自分自身に与え続けなければならない"

江画嶋は書き終り、美人先輩の言葉を考えた。

「普通に、普通に」

二年目の学期末試験で文学の成績は七十四点であった。

十二

「江画嶋、本番だが緊張はないだろう。思い切りやれ。分隊教練は思いどおりに列兵を動かすことが重要だ。気に入らなければ何回でもやり直せ。ゆっくり、ハッキリと指示を出せ。あとは結果が付いてくる。大きな気持、大きな自信、お前は出来る」

「はい、柏田三曹、頑張って来ます」

タタタタタタタ

「受検番号三番、江画嶋士長、実施します」

「はじめ」

「集まれ！」

タタタタ、タータ

「注目！　只今より当分隊の指揮を江画嶋士長が執る、注目直れ。番号！　直れ、揃わない、もう一度実施する。番号！　始め！」

「1」「2」「3」「4」「5」「6」「7」「8」「9」

「只今の番号が各人の固有番号！　只今から停止間および行進間の動作を演練する…」

小部隊の指揮官候補生選考試験は進んでいった。

その後、数ヶ月が経った。

「江画嶋士長、はいります」

「江画嶋士長、候補生指定の内示があった、おめでとう。教育入隊と教育入校は年度をまたぐようだが頑張ってくれ」

「有難うございます。中隊長の御指導のお蔭です」

「夜間大学はどうする、休学届を出すか江画嶋」

「はい、二年間のブランクになりますが、そうしたいと思います。今まで通学への御配慮ありがとうございました」

江画嶋はその日、大学に行った。三年目の通学は数か月で終わることになった。休学届を提出後、気持は一つになった。候補生としての自覚をすることだけだった。

柔らかな時をありがとう。大学キャンパスに別れを告げた江画嶋は帰り掛けに公衆電話を使った。今日の事を故郷の母に伝えたのだ。

この本の文章の中で使用した夏目漱石作品のタイトル一覧

『二百十日』　…春であるが二百十日の…

『三四郎』　…「少しは読んできました。さん、しろー…」

『坊っちゃん』　…「ぼっちゃんと、」

『吾輩は猫である』　…「わがはいはねこであーる、ぐらいは…」

『草枕』　…「…そのためよ。くさまくら…」

『彼岸過迄』　…宵の近づきを感じさせてきた。彼岸過迄とは…

『門』　…慌ただしい時間が終了してキャンパスの門が…

『思い出す事など』　…何も感じるものや、思い出す事などなく、…

『道草』　…見晴展望所で道草を食うなどと…

『行人』　…しなければと、時代の行人気取りの…

『虞美人草』　…ヒナゲシの花を見た。そう、虞美人草を。

『それから』　…直ちに撤収、それから休憩だ。…

『夢十夜』　…眠入ったような感覚だった。夢十夜など…

『硝子戸の中』　…店名を記した電気製品、硝子戸の中に招く…

『下宿』　…「いいえ、下宿を借りて、そこからです」

『文鳥』　…急に文鳥のようなものがチヨ、チヨの…

86

『文学論』　「今日は美人先輩の文学論を聞きたいです」

『温かい夢』　「暖かい夢、夢物語ですかね、小説は」

『霧』　「…霧のロンドン、いや霧の大江町ですね」

『倫敦搭』　「こんなのどお？　夜の霧ロンドン風の街路灯…」

『変化』　「さすがー、僕も一句。変化して…」

『明暗』　「…とっさの判断が明暗をわける武道の…」

『こゝろ』　「…顔はああでも心は美人だから…」

『私の個人主義』　「…授業を受けているのに、私の個人主義かな；」

『手紙』　「…それが孝行というものだよ、手紙を出す…」

『杭夫』　「…完全装備を身につける杭夫ん、ん、高風な；」

『昔』　「…触れたときだ。昔のことを喋っても…」

あとがき

私の感受性が豊かだった頃の、その時代の風景を残したいがためにもこの本を造った。若い時の生き方は各人各様だが、理想の夢と正義感を持ちながら精一杯努力し、人生の次の一歩を目指すのは変わらないだろう。この風景の模様もその一つである。英語版は多くの人に読んでもらうために考えた。

ピーター・フラハティさんに翻訳をお願いした。快く引き受けて頂き感謝の気持ちでいっぱいだ。私と同じ一九四七年、昭和二十二年生まれである。ピーターさんは「二月二十二日の二ばっかりの生まれで、は、は、は」と笑った。「私は九月二十七日、学年ではピーターさんが一年兄貴ですよ」と言って二人で微笑んだ。故郷はアイルランド、二十五歳の時に日本に来日したそうだ。陽気で人なつっこいピーターさんの一つの言葉が印象に残る。「極貧の少年時代だった」が。一九四九年、ピーターさんが二歳の時に独立したアイルランドの社会状況によるものだろうか？　私も貧困は知っている。終戦から数年は戦後の混乱が収まらず、食糧事情など逼迫していた。気持は通じ合う。

もう一つ、互いに夏目漱石ファンだ。特に『草枕』のことでは意気投合している。ピーターさんは「主人公の画工が登場人物たちと交わす会話や個々のシーンの一つひとつが、絵

88

画のように思えた」と言う。舞台となっている天水町小天が美しいのにも由るのだろう。其故に結実された小説だ。近代化に浮かれて伝統や歴史を忘れるなという『草枕』のモチーフが実感できるという。人々は田舎で精いっぱい生きているともいう。『草枕』がアイルランドへの郷愁を呼び起こしている様にも思える。故郷と自然を愛するピーターさんの言葉を深く受け止めて大切にしたい。

最後に、私の師友であるロンドン漱石記念館の館長、恒松郁生氏の示唆でピーター・フラハティさんに翻訳をお願いすることが出来たことを、大変有り難く思っている。

そして、トライ出版の本馬利枝子様には、満足するものを独り善がりで頼み苦労を御掛けした。又、色々な御指導を頂いた。御礼と感謝を申し上げたい。

二〇二四年二月

江上信行

89

著者略歴
江上信行（えがみのぶゆき）
1947 年　熊本県玉名市生まれ。
1967 年　熊本県立玉名高校卒業
　　　　　陸上自衛隊入隊（通信科）
1971 年　熊本短期大学（社会科）卒業
　　　　　熊本商科大学編入（商学部）
1973 年　熊本商科大学中退
2001 年　陸上自衛隊　定年退官
2002 年　崇城大学職員
2014 年　崇城大学定年退職

現在　玉名歴史研究会理事　『歴史玉名』編集委員
　　　くまもと漱石倶楽部会員　熊本城顕彰会会員

著作　『青春昭和映画館』『背番号3』『漱石に秋骨』等
　　　熊日出版
　　　『歴史玉名』第103号　令和5年2月
　　　（夏目漱石の小説『草枕』最終章に出て来る停車場
　　　の実景について）

翻訳者プロフィール
ピーター・フラハティ（Peter Flaherty）
職業　元崇城大学教授
誕生　1947 年生まれ
国籍　アイルランド共和国
来日　1972 年 9 月
職歴　1972 年〜 1974 年　東京で日本語など学習
　　　1974 年〜 1981 年　熊本市や天草で伝道活動と大学
　　　　　　　　　　　　　非常勤講師
　　　1981 年〜 2012 年　崇城大学の専任教員
　　　2012 年〜 2013 年　中国重慶市の四川外国語大学の
　　　　　　　　　　　　　招聘教授
現在　民泊ハウスフォルチェ、英語編集・校正・翻訳
　　　熊本アイルランド協会理事

漱石の名作に恋して

令和六年二月二十二日　発行

著　者　　江上信行

発行者　　小坂拓人

発行所　　株式会社 トライ
　　　　　〒八六一―〇一〇五
　　　　　熊本県熊本市北区植木町味取三七三―一
　　　　　ＴＥＬ　〇九六―二七三―二五八〇

印　刷　　株式会社 トライ

製　本　　日宝綜合製本株式会社

In Love with the Works of
Natsume Soseki

Egami Nobuyuki

Translated by Peter Flaherty

Preface

Natsume Soseki was born and raised in Edo, now Tokyo. The original Edo as the capital of Japan was characterized by economic growth and blossoming cultures. From that historic city, Soseki went forth to teach in Matsuyama and Kumamoto before going to study in London, the capital of England. Inevitably as a proud native of Edo, then moving to live in rural Japan and subsequently in a European metropolis seems to have had a profound influence on Soseki. His experiences and the circumstances he found himself in at times brought with them various levels of anxiety, confusion, and indeed hardship. His experiences gave rise to an abiding sense of curiosity and expectations, yet were frequently mingled with feelings of despair and a censorious attitude, all of which ultimately resulted in his literary masterpieces.

Readers of Soseki are likely to empathise with the humour, and the turmoil resulting from the circumstances and imbalanced states of many of the characters portrayed in his works. Readers will also experience a sense of reassurance as they relate to his description of melancholic and nostalgic incidents which have resonance in their own lives. Readers' emotions will no doubt be aroused by Soseki's unique portrayal of love, family relations, the birth of a child, beautiful scenery, or kindly neighbours as well as less fortunate ones burdened by the iron laws of karmic fate.

Soseki's world resonated with me from the minute I started reading *'Sanshiro'* as the textbook in a Literature class at college. Until then, I was mostly unaware of the forces driving society as well as many of the spiritual aspects of human nature. I was also indifferent to the importance of literature for cultivating

a deeper understanding of our world and one's behaviour.

The depth and dimension of Soseki's literary themes are often reflecting a society in which the four-squared world of common sense has been erased. Soseki's writings delve into and describe three disparate worlds: the nostalgic or tribal milieu of one's hometown, the academic world, and the social setting in which lovely women blossom like the beautiful flowers of spring.

In writing *'In Love with the Works of Natsume Soseki,'* I have tried to intersperse the text with the titles of the principal novels of Soseki. A list of the main works which I drew on is included at the end of this book. I am not sure how much I succeeded in depicting my enthrallment with Soseki through this short story, but it was fun to try. I hope that the reader will also enjoy the story.

Egami Nobuyuki

3

Contents

1

bata-bata-bata-bata, whup-whup-whup, chop-chop,

wubba-lubba, dub-dub, ching-ching, ga-ga

The combined sound of the engine's turbine and rotating propeller is booming and pierces one's ears. Gusts of air accompanying the noise push and toss the stooped body. The tall grass is hissing loudly, making a great fuss as if eager to take the lead. It is spring, but the weather is more akin to *nihyaku toka,* when fierce autumn storms rush through the fields and wipe out the year's crop.

Once the HUIB helicopter landed at the training area in the rolling grassland everything changed suddenly and became entirely different from when the aircraft was in flight. Until it touched down, it seemed as if the helicopter was on a pleasant sightseeing trip. However, from the moment Egashima and his colleagues disembarked, entered the training area, and got into military drill mode, everything became frantic and the helicopter seemed to be like an aircraft involved on the battlefields of Vietnam, as was depicted in recent news footage on the television. Furthermore, even though we had just landed, everyone had to be prepared to take off at once as if in an emergency. As a result, the soldiers became, even more so, worked up and flustered than when doing other duties.

"Egashima and Fujiwara. Are you ready? Start the drills!"

Staff Sergeant Nakamura, leader of Unit 1 of the Multiple Wireless Communications teams, yelled with all his might so that his commands wouldn't get lost in the prevailing commotion. Even so, more than half of what he shouted was drowned out and sounded like the hoarse chirping of some small insect.

5

"Got it!" Egashima responded vigorously.

However, the loudest possible reply that Egashima could make does not even reach the ears of his other team members. The three of them are unloading the considerable amount of equipment on board the helicopter, and rapidly placing devices in a row outside the range of the propeller's rotation circle.

"Hey, you guys are not pumped up enough!   Did the two of you eat? Hurry up! Move! Faster! How is the equipment?"

"The antenna element – is fine. Terminal equipment – is fine also. Wireless devices – all are fine. Next is the Number 1 generator. Let's lift it!"

"Oh, it's so damn heavy! One, two, three," Egashima counts to coordinate his team's efforts.

"Generator 1 – okay.   Next, Number 2. One, two, three. Generator 2 - okay"

"Hey, you guys, don't stop! *Kiai, Kiai,* more fighting spirit, speed up!"

From the sky covered with darkening clouds rain begins to fall, adding greater frenzy to the atmosphere of a simulated battlefield, made all the more realistic through having to perform the fast-paced drills and exercises.

"Ah, good afternoon - oh, good evening! You're having coffee. Can I join you here?"

"Oh, Egashima. Did you have a lecture cancelled, too?"

"No, it's just that I was late. Did *Bijin-senpai* know about the cancellation?"

"*Bijin*? Ooh…? Well, anyhow thanks for speaking the truth. No, I didn't know the class would be cancelled."

"Eh?"

"I came here as usual for the first-period class. The teacher seemingly had

some urgent business to see to, so I suppose cancelling the class was inevitable."

"You have been hanging out here from the start then. I'll stay here too."

"You can't do that. Go and listen to the lecture even if you're late. It's a waste not to."

"No, it's all right. Today's is still only the second lecture. Also, the class has been going on for forty minutes at this stage."

"That's where it's important."

"Even *Bijin-senpai* can sound strict."

"Well, anyway. Coffee… You can drink it here. I've no other choice."

"Even when *Bijin-senpai* speaks like that to me, well, I feel a little bit happy, even if it's coming from a motherly figure two years older than me, ah, no, I mean from a lovely girl!"

"Egashima, you're lucky. Yours is a workplace where you can attend classes on time. I can't do that when we're busy. And no one will substitute for me. Today, I was able to come a little early, and then when I arrived, this is what happens."

"My job is not what you think it is. I can't come to lectures at all when special drills and exercises are being held. That was the case yesterday. Today, I came back from the training area in the afternoon. I can attend classes today because we were able to complete the mission assignment in good time."

"Anyway, you are now here. It seems both of us somehow managed to make it to class today."

Sunlight from the setting sun shines into the stands of trees on the university grounds. With sun rays filtering in from the side, the pure colour of the fresh leaves displays a strong and vivid contrast.

The neat one-story building with a white wall, also lit by the sunlight, is the cafeteria. The interior has simple décor, a pleasant atmosphere, and the type of

background music that is popular with students is always playing. Like the scenery outside, the cafeteria itself has an air of freshness, reflected in the facial expressions and youthful aspirations of the freshmen who have just entered.

Even though the first-period class in the Evening Division is still going on, today there are almost no empty chairs in the cafeteria. Due to the sudden cancellation of the class in Japanese Literature, many of the enrolled students are using the place while waiting for the next lecture. Cancelling classes is essentially not a good thing, especially for diligent students who want to study hard. However, cancelled lectures can serve a slightly different purpose for students who have entered the Evening Division to study after work. The first-period lectures are from 6:00 to 7:30 pm. The free 90 minutes resulting from a cancelled lecture presents a welcome opportunity to soothe away the fatigue of daytime work. The music being played in the cafeteria can also help this recuperation process. If by chance the second-period lecture from 7:40 to 9:10 pm were to be cancelled as well, for some students this extra break would represent pure luxury!

"Egashima, listen carefully! The students belonging to the Evening Division are called "commuting working scholars." So, for them, there are two worlds. The workplace during the day is their practical situation as real members of society, and night school is the place for an idealistic person who strives to find the truth. I may sound arrogant, but I'm happy to experience these two worlds at the same time while I'm still young. This would be impossible without a degree of magnanimity offered by those in charge in the workplace, and attending classes is the only way to repay the favour of being able to take time off from my job, especially when work is busy. But, of course, it takes effort to never miss a class, and sometimes I fear that attending every lecture can become merely a formality. So, come to think of it, I believe that students in the Evening Division try to

justify the break they receive due to a class cancellation as being a good thing simply because it gives a sort of time-out to those who have to study when they are already feeling tired due to work."

"Umm, if I were to simply interpret what *Bijin-senpai* is saying, it seems it might be a good thing if occasionally classes were cancelled."

"In a nutshell, yes, that's it. During such a break, one can read books such as this one I brought with me today."

"Reading it will also help you to prepare for the next lecture. Needless to say, I also bought the textbook. Paperbacks are great because they are not bulky. They are cheaper too. Getting the anthology can wait."

"Well then, you should read the paperback."

"I have read some of it."

"How much did you read?"

"About two pages."

"What? And you understood the whole novel from that?"

"Yes, *Sanshiro* doesn't seem to be a judo story."

"You know, I think I'm a little ahead of you when it comes to Natsume Soseki."

"I knew about '*Botchan*' and '*I Am a Cat*'. I didn't know any other titles. How much did *Bijin-senpai* know?"

"You heard last week that Natsume Soseki stayed in Kumamoto for four years. I knew that long ago. That's why I became interested in the connection between Soseki and Kumamoto. It's also the reason I chose Literature for my elective from among the General Education subjects. The novels '*Kusamakura*' and '*Nihyakutoka*' are also based on Soseki's experience in Kumamoto. So, you should read and study them as well. I call them the '*Soseki Kumamoto Trilogy*.'"

"Just as one might expect! My *Big Senior* was always ahead of me in kindergarten, elementary school, junior high school, and senior high school. How excellent and reliable she always seemed to be! As Literature is the only subject I'm taking with *Bijin-senpai* at college, I'll give it my best."

"Will you please stop calling me *Bijin-senpai* and *Big Senior*?"

"Oh, there's no need to get worked up. I'm doing it for free!"

"Well, OK then. I suppose being addressed that way by a cute junior is tolerable. I'll remind myself Egashima is calling me that way out of appreciation."

"That's how it should be. By the way, in last week's explanatory lecture about the course, Professor Kamachi mentioned that he would ask students one by one to read sentences from *Sanshiro*. It would be embarrassing if one were to read a kanji incorrectly."

"Don't worry, he won't ask you to read."

"Why do you think so? Is it because there are so many students taking his lectures?

"Yes, that's part of it, but the teacher only asks students who are likely to be able to read the sentences correctly."

"Well, in that case, I'm unlikely to lose face."

Looking out the window of the cafeteria, it's clear that the evening is closing in. It is said that the *higan* marks the end of both the best of summer and the worst of winter. However, without any reference to the Spring *higan*, when the students enter college in April, the brightness of the evening varies depending on the weather. On cloudy and rainy days, the difference from sunny days is rather extreme. As May and June pass, this difference becomes less, and classes in the first period are usually held with the sunlight coming through the windows. This continues until the summer vacation starts in July. Soon after the second

semester begins in September, however, the brightness suddenly gets shorter. And from late autumn, it's completely dark by the time the first-period lecture begins.

Sensitive to such seasonal changes, students in the Evening Division spend three hours every day on campus, except for Sundays and national holidays. The 10-minute break between the first and second periods is usually taken up with moving to another lecture room. After these hectic hours are over and students walk out the gates of the campus, within minutes their minds and bodies start getting ready for the next day at work.

Naturally, students in the Evening Division will make an effort to talk to other students during the limited time available. Creating such opportunities to engage in conversations is often a priority for them, and chatting can become a valuable source of enjoyment.

"*Bijin-senpai,* Lecture Room 333 is waiting for you. Let's go to meet Natsume Soseki."

"Oh, it's that time! "*I'm a Beautiful Cat!*" How does that strike you?"

Lecture Room 333 is already full of students. Mostly female students enroll in the Literature class, which is an elective subject. The number of male students is small when compared with other General Education courses. Little wonder then that none of Egashima's colleagues had chosen to enroll in the Literature class.

The first lecture, held the previous week, focused on how to apply Literature to one's career as well as on some approaches to studying literary works. The teacher gave a brief overview of the relationship between Natsume Soseki and Kumamoto, and several classes concentrating on reading *Sanshiro* were to start today. *Sanshiro* is based on a student whom Soseki had taught in Kumamoto.

"Egashima, you sit over there."

"There are only women sitting there. What about you *Biji-senpai?*"

"I'll sit next to that classmate at the back."

"I'd rather be in the back too."

"You can't do that. Younger students are supposed to sit in the front. Up there they also might have good things happen to them."

"Such as being asked to read?"

"No, that's not it."

Egashima decided to listen to his senior and reluctantly took a seat in the front. Unlike other subjects where he sat side by side with male students, he felt that he was out of place here. On the other hand, he was oddly pleased that he could not choose a seat so as to avoid contact with women.

Facing the podium, the only vacant seat in the front section was the outermost seat in the third row, on the right side of the middle aisle. Looking at it from the podium, the vacant seat was right in front of the teacher. It seemed as if this seat was left that way to make it easy to sit in. Egashima sat down there. After putting his notebook and the *Sanshiro* paperback on the desk, he took a quick look around the classroom. Feeling a little bit ill at ease, he realized he had sat down in a seat that was not entirely to his likening. He soon turned his head and body to look at the seats behind him. In the last row, on the left side of the middle aisle, in the first seat from the inside, Egashima could see the face of his senior who was talking happily to the classmate sitting beside her.

Egashima chuckled to himself that these two chatting females would never appear as heroines in any kind of literary story. While lightheartedly toying with this impression, he started to reflect on his own life so far. His interests lay only in reading manga magazines or daydreaming about scenes he had seen in movies. For Egashima, reading novels was similar to having to do a task that was not really necessary to survive or make a living.

Naturally, for Egashima, who worked in the rough atmosphere of a men's organization where intuition and wits matter, the Literature class about to start could hardly be expected to elicit any special memories, feelings, or inspiration. Literature was merely an academic subject in which a student could earn one of the credits necessary to complete college education and graduate.

Professor Kamachi entered the classroom and stood on the podium in front of the blackboard. He placed the thick anthology in his hand on the desk and bowed lightly. The noisy lecture hall suddenly became quiet. The professor stood for a few seconds and looked around the classroom before speaking. All the students watched and listened attentively for his first words. The classroom was soundless and quiet, with a stillness that almost doused the wavelength tones of the lit fluorescent lights.

"Is everyone breathing?"

At that moment, a burst of laughter erupted in the classroom. Then, as soon as the teacher began to talk, those attending the lecture were drawn into the world of Natsume Soseki by the professor's skillful storytelling.

< *When he woke up, he saw that the woman had struck up a conversation with the old man seated next to her.... Sanshirō and the woman had been riding together since Kyōto* >

At the beginning of a lecture, the professor himself usually started to read some section from a novel. When he began reading from the introductory part of *Sanshiro,* the eyes of the student audience gradually shifted from the teacher standing on the podium to the script on the printed paper in front of them.

<.......... Her dark complexion had caught his eye as soon as she boarded. Once Sanshiro left Kyūshū and transferred to the Sanyō line, he noticed that women grow fairer in colour as he approached the Kyōto-Ōsaka region. It increased his awareness of having left home, and he felt a tinge of sadness. The woman's presence in the car was comforting, as though he had found a compatriot of the opposite sex. Her skin tone was unmistakably southern and of Kyushu>

Professor Kamachi stopped reading the text there and began to describe in rakugo style the next scene in the story, in which the main character Sanshiro and the woman are staying at an inn for the night. Suddenly, the professor raised his right index finger, took aim, and stretched out his right arm.

"You there, you the boy sitting in the flower garden of ladies. Read the next scene. Loudly, that is."

The words startled Egashima. He looked around to confirm that he was the person who was supposed to read aloud. He was the only man seated in that section. Furthermore, the teacher's eyes and index finger were pointing directly at him. Astonished, Egashima looked around him for the second time. Students in the front looked back with a grin or a smirk, while others seemed to commiserate with him. Those to his left and right stuck out their heads to get a peek at him. The whole room stirred slightly.

Egashima, who had never liked having to stand up and read aloud since elementary school, braced himself. He should be glad to have been designated the first reader of this year's Literature class. This was his chance to relish the honour of such a memorable occasion. But somehow he felt in a bind. How should he read? At work during the day, he always speaks loudly and is required to be

precise. Should he read as if he is in that same kind of atmosphere? To him reading in a weak voice would be completely out of tune. Anyway, he decided to remove his body from the chair and stood up in that spot. Two students in the back row clapped their hands. Many of the students sitting around Egashima also burst into applause as if in accompaniment with the two female students clapping at the back.

"Shush! This is the first recitation of the year. It is a special moment. Be quiet, and listen," Professor Kamachi admonished the class.

At the professor's words, Egashima sought to control his nerves. As the room fell silent, Egashima prepared to read slowly and clearly. Previously he had a premonition that he might be called on to do something like this, but he was dumbfounded that the occasion had come so early in the course. He hadn't done any preparation for reading the ideographs that appeared in the text. He had just skimmed through the commentary on the story. Lacking sufficient confidence to read perfectly, Egashima urged himself to "Calm down, calm down!" His lack of guts appalled him and he was worried that his voice might start to tremble. How loud should he read?

Maybe it would be good enough just to be heard by the teacher. Anyhow, here goes:

<When they arrived at the station, the woman told Sanshirō that she would be taking the Kansai Line toward Yokkaichi. Sanshirō's train was due to arrive shortly. The woman still had some time to wait for hers, so she accompanied him as far as the ticket gate. "Sorry for imposing too much on you. Have a safe trip and good luck." She bowed her head to him graciously. Sanshirō held his leather bag and umbrella in the left hand, removed his cap with the other, and said simply,

"Goodbye." The woman was //////////.....>

Egashima heard *"unblinkingly"* whispered from beside him. He started to re-read from where he had gotten stuck.

<The woman was unblinkingly gazing at his face, and then commented in a casual tone. "Not a ladies' man, are you?" She grinned at him mischievously. Sanshirō felt as though he'd been hurled out onto the platform. When he re-entered the train car ...>

"As far as there!"

At the professor's direction, Egashima stopped reading. He felt relieved and as though he had fulfilled a very important duty.

"Yes, that was pretty good. You sounded like the main character himself!"

Weird feelings seemed to swell inside Egashima once more. "Oh, why do I feel a bit excited at merely having read a few sentences aloud?" he lamented to himself. The professor continued with the lecture, but Egashima just could not concentrate for the moment. He quickly tried to regain his composure and then turned his face halfway to look sideways at the student beside him who had taught him how to read the kanji he didn't know. She was just looking straight ahead intently.

After the lecture ended, everyone started moving all at once. Egashima quickly turned his head to the right. The girl student who had been sitting next to him had also left her seat and was chatting animatedly with the student who had sat in front of them.

2

hum-hum-hum, buzz-buzz, duh, du-, du,

The field generator starts to emit a dull rotating sound and then grinds to a halt without reaching the normal operational speed of 3,600 revolutions. Even when the starter cord is pulled a dozen times, the device still will not start.

"Leading Private Tanaka, there's no use pulling it. It just won't start."

"Brush the spark plugs one more time then."

"This machine is hard to handle because devices such as these are manufactured in such a clumsy manner."

"What are you talking about, Egashima? Your pull on the cord is just too weak. That's why it won't rotate! Here, let me pull it…. *doh, doo, doo, hum-hum-hum.* …See? It's up and running again!"

"Yes, indeed. Three bowls of rice a day make all the difference!"

"Egashima, don't just stand there lost in admiration! Hurry up and test the voltage and transmission capacity."

"Yes, Sir. Yes, Sir!"

"What's wrong with both of you guys? If you don't speed things up, we won't make it in time for the radio wave transmission."

"Don't worry, Master Sergeant Hanada. The necessary preparations at our local field station have all been completed smoothly."

"Is that so? Sergeant Yamazaki at the sub-station site is also all set up for transmitting the relay signals. Have you checked the frequency meter and antenna?"

"Yes, all done."

"Okay then. Start the radio waves transmission."

"Okay, I'll start now."

"The reception level and sensitivity are both good. Detection between the B terminal and the relay exchange point is also fine. We'll have to calibrate the circuit network with the B terminal."

Tanaka and Egashima quickly managed to complete the frequency adjustment and detection levels of their wireless team with those of their counterparts at the signal reception terminal. Tanaka reported on the operations in a loud voice from inside the communication shelter to Leading Private Tanaka, who was supervising the outside procedures.

"Every channel is operating as normal. Staff Sergeant Nakamura's route seems to have finished too. OK, then. Withdraw the assembled meshes from the circuit lines and shut the instruments down. After collecting all of the equipment, put it in the storehouse. In five minutes, gather in there and I'll explain the next drills."

Tanaka turned to Egashima with a smile on his face.

"Egashima, you'll be able to go to college today in time for class."

"Yes, it's all thanks to you!"

"Come on, Egashima, you worked hard, too."

Things can get somewhat hectic at the gates in front of the university in the evening. Buses operated by several different transport companies that serve different routes line up to disgorge and take on passengers. These buses are used mostly by students who are commuting to and from college. So, when the students in the Evening Division get off the bus, the regular daytime students are waiting to get on.

The moment the working students get off the crowded buses and breathe in the outside air they feel a lightness of mind and body. The main entrance of the university is right beside the bus stop. The height of the gates is much lower than the stone pillars on either side of the entrance. Students enter through the gates onto an approach avenue that is lined with ginkgo trees. While mixing with

daytime students on their way out from the university, those engaged in full-time work are at once transformed into night students. On the campus, there are lots of facilities waiting to welcome them as well as to absorb their minds.

At the end of the tree-lined avenue, there is a ginkgo tree, which is poised as if it were a king proudly watching over the trees directly in front of it. Right behind it, the side wall of Building No. 5 serves as a backdrop for this tree. The drabness of its rough cement wall is a testament to the advanced age of this building. The lordly ginkgo tree and the two-story Building No 5 are the starting point for the road to diverge to the left or the right.

The road to the right is the only road on campus coloured with paint. There is a row of lecture halls along its route. Students using this road call it "Main Street." On the right-hand side of it, there's the old gymnasium which is due to be demolished and one can also notice that preparations are already underway for the construction of a new one.

Following on from there is the four-story Building No. 4, the three-story Building No. 1, and then the Library. Students also use this part of the campus as a place for relaxation or hanging out with friends.

On the left side of the library, there is a one-story large auditorium with a roofed lobby extending from it. This lobby also serves as a corridor that is connected to the first-floor entrance of Building No. 1. Inside the lobby there's a noticeboard attached to the wall.

The four-story Building No. 3 is behind the auditorium and on its first floor is the student cafeteria. The third floor of Building No.1, the second floor of Building 3, and the reading room on the second floor of the library are connected by a passageway called "the modern bridge," so it is possible to come and go between any of these buildings without having to pass through the separate main entrances.

Since the area below the bridge serves as a passageway to the first floor of four buildings, the lobby section of the corridor becomes a pivotal central base. Egashima calls it the "*encounter lobby*."

This part of the campus accommodates the core facilities of the university, and in front of Building No. 1, in which the university's headquarters are located, there is both a beautiful circular miniature garden and a triangular one.

A large playground that can easily facilitate track and field events, baseball, and volleyball matches, spreads out in front of the core facilities, and from here students are afforded a panoramic view of the rows of poplar trees that surround the entire site.

Turning to the left at the fork where the road diverges, there are two lecture halls, standing together on the left side. These are Buildings No 6 and No 7. As well as being two-story, both buildings look the same as the aged Building No 5. Behind them, there is a gymnasium, in front of which are three tennis courts and a swimming pool complete with a high diving platform.

The working adult students regard their time and the facilities on the large campus as offering them the freedom and opportunity to train both the body and the mind.

Egashima got off the bus with his two colleagues. The three of them walked about five paces distant and arrived at the notice board in the lobby a few seconds apart. Looking at the bulletin board and reading about the content of the first physical education class, they learn that the curriculum will consist mainly of practical exercises. "Since we do more than enough physical activities at work, there is really no need for these physical education classes," they commiserate with each other while looking somewhat resentfully at the notice board.

The gymnasium is small and dark, and six circular concrete pillars with a diameter of one meter take up valuable space. Calling it a military facility rather than a college gym would seem quite appropriate. However, until the new gymnasium is completed, indoor gymnastics are to be held there. At the orientation class, the instructor said that although the gymnasium might not be suitable for some events, he intended to hold creative classes that would satisfy the needs and wishes of all the students.

Egashima, after attending the first-period class in Building No. 2, returned to

the lobby. The female senior whom Egashima admires and is fond of was there. She is two years older than Egashima. When she was in high school, her homeroom teacher encouraged her to go on to university, but due to family circumstances, she had no choice but to give up thoughts of going to college and she started working immediately after graduating from high school. But four years later, she says her renewed desire to learn is driving her to attend night school. When he enlisted in the Self-Defense Forces, due to the locations of military exercises as well as having been transferred several times, Egashima didn't have the opportunity to enroll in a higher education institution. So, he had to enter college three years behind students of the same age. The female senior entered college ahead of him, leaving them one year apart.

"Egashima, what's your next class?"

"It's physical education."

"Wouldn't it be enough if you only answered the attendance roll call? After all, you're always conditioning your body through your job," she suggested mischievously. Regarding her as a person who understood his way of life, Egashima earnestly replied, "Well, the body is the source of my income."

"And the head doesn't matter," she shot straight back.

"Well, yes and no, or even maybe so," Egashima responded.

Then almost at once, "Oh, I'm sorry. I was just joking," she said with a slight giggle.

Then she continued.

"Your ways of thinking and doing things might be fine while you're still young. What I'd like to say to you is the same as what I tried to tell you last week. Your youthful idealism is all about strengthening the body and mind. You work hard to train your body at a day job and then you try to cultivate your mind at university at night. What do you think of what I'm saying?"

"Just what I would expect from *Bijin-senpai!* Thank you for your wonderful thoughts and words again today."

"You're aiming to distinguish yourself, to achieve excellence in both martial

and liberal arts, the magnificent twin swords of science and literature! Oh, but how to achieve the perfect balance? In other words, find that elusive equilibrium. That's the crucial and practical issue in your life at present."

"You're getting more and more admirable, my Big Senior!"

"See you in Literature class tomorrow."

After standing and chatting together, Egashima watched his senior as she hurried to the next lecture hall. She had that type of mindset and personality that enabled her to give sound advice. She would be perfect for the role of the strong-willed mother in movies or TV dramas. From the senior's point of view, Egashima was like a younger brother who listens to anything she says. Meeting each other on campus felt the same as if they were back in their hometown.

On his way to the gymnasium, his two colleagues chased after Egashima. All three of them worked at the same base but in different occupations. However, they are close colleagues who connect easily when discussing work-related grievances or other matters of mutual interest. As colleagues, there's an up-to-date and quick flow of information among them but they realize that such a relationship could also have its drawbacks. If it were always just the three of them interacting with each other, then university life could easily end up being merely an extension of their daytime working place.

The mutual understanding of the three colleagues was that the time spent at the university was something infinitely different from their daytime work hours. This viewpoint was the basis for their relationship on campus. Attending college should consist of behaviour that neutralizes life at the military base was their catchphrase. This they concluded was the real and overriding benefit of being a commuting working scholar. Based on this reasoning, the three of them had agreed to make sure that they would not hang out together on campus, and not even sit close to one another in the same classroom.

But now the two colleagues had lined up on both sides of Egashima.

"Egashima-kun, let's go to the gym together."

"Oh! Niina-kun and Matsuo-kun, let's do that".

As soon as the three of them started walking side by side, their thoughts also seemed to mesh and they agreed to meet at the end of the physical education class. Egashima and his two colleagues were enrolled in different majors, so practical skills classes were held on separate days. However, because today was the first class of the physical education course and was devoted to physical fitness tests and bodily measurements, they had to attend class at the same time in the gymnasium.

Measuring pulse rates after a series of exercises, assessing the body's flexibility, zigzag dribbling, and other tasks proved easy for Egashima, but he felt a sense of novelty when doing movements that he normally didn't perform. Each group included female participants also. As students completed the various tests, conversations with other members of their group gradually increased, and it became an entertaining physical education class. Those who finished an evaluation test had time to observe other groups while waiting for the next task. Egashima watched various other groups going through their exercises.

Egashima suddenly noticed the girl who had taught him how to read a kanji during the previous Literature class. He hadn't been aware of her at all during the attendance roll call at the beginning of class. Now she was climbing up and down on a platform, her hair streaming in rhythm with the shouts of encouragement from her group. Egashima watched her movements until she finished her tests.

When the class finished, Egashima and his two colleagues left the gymnasium together. There were many routes from the gymnasium to the main gates, but most students as a matter of course headed to the main gates by turning at the bright Building No 4.

"Let's march abreast on the tree-lined street!"

The three of them lined up side by side and began counting their steps from the front of the kingly ginkgo tree while keeping a steady pace.

"One hundred and ninety steps."

"Matsuo, Niina, how many meters?"

"Yes, General Egashima, 133 meters."

The three of them burst out laughing at the same time.

The bus for home soon arrived at their stop.

clippety-clop, scrunch-scrunch, crunch-crunch, gasp-gasp, kata-kata, argh

"Hey, you're going to be overtaken! Swing those arms faster and bend your elbows a bit more. Hang in there – you're almost finished!"

Egashima was quite desperate. Even though he was going all out following team leader Sergeant Tsuji's encouragement, his legs just would not move the way he wanted. His body felt heavy and sluggish. The team behind was catching up on him. To make things worse, his stomach started to hurt. He wonders if he ate too much for lunch. The finish line is still quite a distance away. The race between teams while carrying equipment is an endurance test where the challenge for competing units is to reach the camp gate first and be declared the winner.

The race is a round trip of some five kilometres to and from the top of Mt. Tatsuta, which is 152 meters above sea level. So, the race is a real battle of physical strength and endurance for the participating units. For Egashima, because personal honour as well as that of his Multiple Radio Communication unit is at stake, the endurance test means that far more energy and grit are required than are usually demanded in other types of military exercises.

Tatsuta is not a high mountain, but the runners have to go up a narrow and steep animal trail from the middle of the climb. Taking the gentle slope through the park road is prohibited. Playful gestures such as eating grass on the wayside and the verges at the observation platform, doing a double round of the triangular table at the apex before starting to descend, and then running down through the residential area were slight deviations that relieved the tedium of having to just keep on running and running. Of the four rival units, not a single runner failed to reach the south gate of the camp. His superior, Second Lieutenant Murakami, said to Egashima: "You did a great job. Wipe off your sweat and prepare for the next exercise. And make sure you don't fall asleep during your night class at the university!"

Beyond the front exit of the base where Egashima is stationed, there is a road lined with cherry blossom trees that are several decades old. These rows also extend from quite some distance inside the base, so when the trees are in full bloom, the vista is like a decorated stretch that follows the undulations of the countryside far into the distance. At the bottom of this slope, is the Kikuchi train track with a major road running parallel to it. Egashima crosses the train track and boards the bus at the adjacent roadside stop. The bus route traverses through wide and narrow prefectural roadways, a congested national route, and local municipal alleys. When the bus reaches the tracks of the electric streetcar, Egashima gets off at the Yakuencho stop. A stone wall runs along the side of the road and serves as the boundary of a temple compound. The wall is both quite high and wide and on its top, several billboards advertising movies are displayed in a way that will best attract people's attention. Egashima walks about 150 meters along the road to the stop from which the bus to his university departs.

This part of the city has a tram terminal as well as the Kokai market and shopping area, which is known familiarly as the "Citizens' Kitchen." This locality is also regarded as a student quarter with young people engendering a lively and buzzing atmosphere. Egashima, who was born in a rural setting often feels a little bit on edge here while waiting for the bus and consequently forgets about how tired he is following his day's work at the base.

Egashima's bus to the university goes diagonally to the right at the V-shaped intersection and crosses a bridge with an elliptical arch. Here, there are good views both to the left and right due to the open space around the river. After crossing the bridge, the next street goes down through a part of the inner city. From there, gaining speed as if eager to help student passengers get on with their learning, the bus goes directly to the front of the university. Egashima gradually comes to regard his commute as a process of self-growth. Exiting the solid iron gates of the military base was a brief liberation from the daily regimentation, constant commands, and training drills. Riding the bus on busy urban roads was a kind of social mobility on the way to a better life. The final stage of entering the

soothing realm of academia opened up a path to learning new things and forming dreams. Egashima often felt deep satisfaction at being a commuting working scholar.

< *Sanshiro remained still and studied the pond's surface. A myriad of large trees was reflected in its depths, and deeper still was an image of the blue sky. Then, a feeling of desolation came upon Sanshiro, as he imagined himself riding the train to school.....During his high school days in Kumamoto, he'd often hike into the Tatsuta hills, where it was much quieter than here..... Now Sanshiro wasn't thinking about trains, or Tōkyō, or even Japan. His thoughts were distant and far removed.....>*

On reading this passage in *Sanshiro*, Egashima realizes that the bus stop he transfers to at Yakuencho is near the high school where Sanshiro had studied. That Tatsuta in particular is mentioned in the novel left an impression on him. The lovely hills of Tatsuta, or more correctly Mount Tatsuta, are quite close to Egashima's camp and workplace. He frequently has had to run up and down this mountain as part of his physical training. If Soseki himself climbed it, then Egashima would have to think more about Mt. Tatsuta and those wayfarers in the Meiji era of the author's time. At the same time, Egashima once again felt dismayed at his ignorance and how unconcerned with such topics his life so far had been.

One Sunday, Egashima left the camp alone and climbed Mt. Tatsuta. He looked down at the city from the spot which had the best view. Shifting his gaze, he identified two university buildings by their height and size, among an expansive group of black tiled roofs. "Aah, literature! Aah, Soseki, Soseki!" Egashima let out a deep sigh.

Sitting on a bench at the apex, Egashima dozed off for a short while in the gentle breeze. As he ambled down the mountain, he noticed a flower with six petals on a solitary stalk. "Oh, a field poppy!" he chuckled to himself.

4

thump-thump, pound-pound, thwack-thwack,

"Are the stakes driven firmly into the ground? Are the poles connected? Are all the side wires attached and in a good position? Are the antenna apparatuses and the wave polarization correctly orientated? Is there any slack at the end of the connection cable?"

"Everything is all set, Sir"

"Roger. Raise the antennas!"

"Hey, can't you see it's going up diagonally, - pay more attention!"

The iron stakes pounded into the ground with a sledgehammer, metal pipes combined in layers, weaving branch wires like a spider's web, and two communication towers built to transmit and receive signals are standing as if reaching for the sky.

bonk, clunk

"The first antenna works well. The second one is fine also."

thump, plonk

"Okay, I'll correct the tilt."

"That seems fine now."

"Tilt corrected, the direction set and the antennas are up and working well."

Second Lieutenant Aoki, the platoon leader, had a grim expression on his face during the whole drill.

"You're too slow, it took too long, and even the basics are out of sync. Dismantle the apparatuses at once. We'll take a break, and then we'll repeat the drills for putting up the poles and antennas properly."

"Got it."

"Start dismantling the equipment. Go to it, action, fast!" the unit leader, Sergeant Shimayama, yells, his sweaty face wrung in a devil-may-care attitude.

Egashima began to croon a verse from a popular song, *"Look up in the*

Sky."

"Hai, - In the big, big sky - Build an antenna in the sky – Build…"

Egashima just managed to get to the classroom in time for the third lecture in Literature because the previous one had run slightly overtime, thus cutting short the break between classes. The room was almost full again this week, but Egashima managed to get a vacant seat near the back. Within ten minutes after the beginning of the lecture, several students in turn had been asked to read aloud from the text.

<As Sanshiro raised his eyes, he saw two women standing atop the rise to his left. They stood near the edge of the pond, and across from where they stood was a tall and thickly-wooded slope. A Gothic-style building clad in bright red brick was behind the hilltop. The setting sun was casting its rays obliquely from beyond the woods and buildings on the far side. The women stood facing the setting sun. Seen from the low shadows where Sanshirō is crouching…>

Egashima's eyes turned away from the printed page and he looked toward the front section and the seat in which he had sat for the previous lecture. Recalling his experience on that occasion he quickly blinked his eyes a couple of times before going back to look at the text.

<As if on cue, the two women walked down together at a leisurely pace…… … She had a small white flower in her left hand and was sniffing it as she approached. Her attention was on the flower under her nose, so she walked with her eyes cast downward. She came to a stop a few meters from Sanshirō. While saying……she lifted her gaze. Then she took one look at Sanshiro. He suddenly became conscious of the movement of the black pupils of the woman's eyes>

Egashima hadn't done any preparation for this lesson nor had he read the

story in advance. His hand lifted the paperback textbook a little toward his face.

<The two women passed in front of Sanshirō. The younger one, who'd been sniffing the white flower, dropped it in front of him as she went by. He gazed after them as they moved away. The nurse walked ahead, with the younger woman following behind. Among the bright hues on her dress, he could see the obi sash, which had various outlines dyed lightly on the base white fabric. She wore a single rose of pure white in her hair. In the shade under the oak branches, the rose had shone prominently among her dark hair locks.>

"How about that scene? This is an account of the first meeting between Sanshiro and Mineko. The story develops from this point. I will continue the lecture by focusing on these two people as well as the social background of the Meiji period. Ah, how I would love to be young again!"

As the professor spoke, the heretofore quiet atmosphere suddenly became more animated.

"After this scene, the two of them won't see each other again for a while. This is how a good writer tantalizes the reader. The reader wants to know when they will meet, but the author instead goes about describing other characters in the story or the various things in the surrounding town. For example, trains....."

Egashima suddenly recalled the first time he and a friend had ridden a train by themselves. It was during the autumn of their first year in junior high school. They got on the electric streetcar in front of the Japan National Railway Station in Kumamoto, but they didn't know which stop was the correct one to get off at. Egashima's friend became a bit flustered and shouted, "I want to go the department store, so let me get off there." Other passengers began to laugh. That day, Egashima and his friend also climbed the new Kumamoto Castle tower, which had just been reconstructed. Egashima felt proud of being able to study at a university in a city with a castle and where streetcars ran.

<The new school year started on September 11th. Sanshirō faithfully went to the university at the appointed time, arriving around 10:30 a.m....>

Professor Kamachi started talking again.

"Did you notice? At the time this novel was written, the academic year also began in the autumn of Japan. If you read the story carefully, it's interesting to discover the novel is not just about the relationship between a man and a woman. I will touch on these matters as we continue our study."

<.........Sanshiro made his way down to the edge of the pond and crouched down again in his usual spot by the oak tree. He imagined that maybe the young lady would stroll by again. He looked up toward the top of the hill several times, but there was no sign of anyone.
.... Sanshiro decided it was time he headed back to his dormitory.>

"In next week's lecture, I would like to put aside the relationship between Sanshiro and the woman and instead talk about Soseki and his time in Kumamoto. During his stay here, Soseki composed some 40% or 955 of his haiku poems. When learning about Soseki, this, too, is an important aspect of his life that is worth examining. The week after next, I'll start from where Sanshiro and the woman meet again for the second time."

The professor finished the lecture at that point and left the classroom.

Egashima closed his book and immediately went out into the hallway to wait for his female senior. She didn't appear for quite some time as she was still talking to her classmates. While waiting there, the student who had helped Egashima read the difficult kanji passed him. She too was engaged in conversation with other students. Just then Egashima heard a voice he recognized talking to him from behind.

"Egashima-senpai, who are you waiting for?"

Egashima turned round. It was his junior, Oyama. He was not enrolled in the

Literature class. After high school, Oyama remained in his hometown and worked as an assistant to his father, a carpenter. At the same time, he also attended classes in the Evening Division and commuted to school by train and bus. Tonight, he had just finished a class in the room next to Egashima's.

"Oh, Oyama. I'm waiting for my senpai."

"Oh, I see. No doubt you mean our big senior from junior high and high school. I heard that the homeroom teacher in high school told her to aim high and become a medical doctor. I don't think that occupation would suit her though!"

"Oh, don't you? Well, I'll tell her what you've just said!"

"No, don't do that! Sure, the three of us are good friends. I should have enrolled in Literature too. It would have been fun if the three of us were there together and could sit side by side."

"Yeah, that's right. You know she could teach us so much. It's one of the benefits of being older."

"Come to think of it, in the Evening Division classes there is a wide range of ages, from students in their forties to those who are only eighteen or nineteen. So, we have the chance to learn in a wonderful academic atmosphere simply by becoming friends with other students."

"Yes, it's a magnificent environment in many ways. Even our juniors can teach us so many things."

"Egashima-senpai, you shouldn't talk about age to our great senior."

"You're right. I'm also in the older age bracket. "

The female senior came out into the hallway while Egashima and Oyama were standing chatting. She seemed overjoyed to see her two juniors together, waved her hand, and greeted them with a huge smile.

"Ah, the premonitions of love, the premonitions of love! Oh, you two guys are so cool and interesting."

"Great Senpai, what's going on here?" Oyama asked in surprise.

"Oyama. *Bijin-senpai* is just quoting from a novel."

"Egashima-senpai, oh I so regret not having chosen Literature as well."

The three of them left Building No 3 and went through the lobby. In addition to the ordinary lighting, there is a special spot lamp there that comes on after dark. It seems to enhance the appearance of those who congregate in the lobby at night. Many students take a short rest here after classes have finished. It also serves as a useful place to find someone to travel home with.

"Any notice of cancelled classes? Um, no, ah, that's too bad."

While looking at the notice board, Egashima and Oyama glance at each other and laugh at the antics of their female senior.

Students heading for the exit usually leave by the main street. The sports ground spreads out to the right of this street and its farther end is wrapped in darkness. The nearer section of the sports ground contains the water drainage area.

Egashima and Oyama listen in silence to their senior who is walking between them and chattering about various things. Whether walking hurriedly or ambling along chatting, like most students from the Evening Division they are heading for the exit, along the tree-lined avenue towards the bus stop right beside the university entrance.

"For you guys, I think this is the time when you feel most fulfilled. You've finished your day job, attended your lectures, and you feel satisfied that you have put in a good day's work."

"Well, now that you mention it, that's very true. So often, on days like these, I feel I scarcely have had a chance to breathe."

"Egashima, that's a bit of an exaggeration. Surely you can't be content with your life as it is right now. Adolescents like us must have dreams for the future and also we should plan carefully on how to reach our goals. The daytime students had to study so hard to pass the entrance exam because of the fierce competition. That's hardly the case for you guys, as the competition to enter the Evening Division is really not all that difficult. So, you shouldn't think that merely attending classes is sufficient. Learning is not just about going to college, you know. Those who reach the top need not only academic qualifications and

expertise but also a wide range of general knowledge. Cultivating one's mental faculties broadens the mind and is a key means of preparing for the future. The same goes for you, Oyama."

"Great Senpai, are you suggesting that erudition is necessary even for a carpenter?"

"Of course, it is! Think of yourself as an architect and not merely a carpenter. In the future, you'll have protégés and you will need to be in a position to guide them."

After exiting the tree-lined street, Egashima and Oyama walked across the pedestrian bridge to the left of the entrance to the bus stop on the opposite side of the road. The female senior, instead of crossing the pedestrian bridge, went to the bus stop at which Egashima had arrived earlier that evening.

The bus that Egashima and Oyama were boarding was heading to Kami-Kumamoto Station. Egashima got off on the way to transfer to the bus for his camp, while Oyama continued straight on. Kami-Kumamoto is the same station at which Natsume Soseki arrived, got off the train, and stepped onto Kumamoto soil for the first time.

bang-bang, bang-bang, bang-bang,

"Get up, get up!"

"This is not a drill. Assemble in the corridor immediately. In-house Team Leaders, check and report on your situation and personnel."

.   "In-house No 2, no abnormalities."

"In-house No 1, no…there are no….

"Good. Conditions are normal. You'll be contacted when things become clearer. It's 2:30 a.m. now. I've received instructions from the commander on night duty. There was an earthquake not too far distant a short while ago and we received orders to stand by in case of having to assist with disaster relief measures. The senior member of each unit should take charge until the Squad Leader arrives, and get ready to depart at a moment's notice. The scale of the disaster, the duration of the response period, and the state of the communications network are still completely unknown. Make every effort to prepare. Fall out."

Since Egashima had returned from college he felt tired and drowsy. Moreover, when the order to get up was given he had just fallen asleep. He was now woken up without having dreamed even a single dream and a far cry from the peaceful ten nights of dreams that he longed for. He listened to what was going on around him while half in a daze and even though he was standing still, his body felt like it was swaying as if in a tremor.

Egashima was selected as a member of the first response team and they departed from the camp before dawn. A few hours later, they arrived in the disaster-stricken area and immediately set up a command post for radio communication and then quickly began to transmit information on local conditions. At the same time, they started laying the ground for the arrival of the main relief force.

The units due to arrive subsequently were supposed to bring necessities

such as food and water for the initial response team. Additional fuel for the power supply of the communication equipment would also need to be delivered later. The initial response team itself had brought only the minimum requirements necessary to commence immediate action. The key priority of this unit was to establish reliable communication means between the stricken area and central command as quickly as possible.

"Egashima and Katsueda, did you bring bottles of water?"

"Yes, full ones, too."

"What about rice cans and dry bread?"

"Yes, we brought the minimum amount needed for a few days. I haven't forgotten Sergeant Kuroki's share either."

"Thank you. Anyhow, let's give it our best."

"Aye."

"Aye."

"Egashima, you're lucky to have been selected for the leading response team. This kind of relief work might involve a long-term engagement with other units. Thanks to the Squad Leader's consideration you will be able to continue commuting to college."

Egashima was hugely relieved on hearing this.

The telecommunications team, under the supervision of Uemura, was taxed with putting up telephone wires in the worst-hit places. Following deployment, these would enable each unit to start using field telephones.

A short time later a message came in for Sergeant Kuroki. He was informed that due to static noise interfering with the caller's voice, transmissions on these phones were unclear and needed to be improved.

"Egashima and Katsueda: I was told that every channel seems to be of poor quality. We have to reset the antennas. The Kobashi amplitude modulation unit discovered that their location was too restrictive and was ordered to move the communication equipment to a different position. Shin Inoue from The Telegraph Group identified the problem and immediately proposed a potential solution. We

have to move both the transmission and reception wire poles. If that doesn't work out, we would need to try another site. Setting up reliable methods for core communication involves great difficulties and is a huge responsibility."

"OK. I clearly understand our situation."

After eating rice curry at the student's cafeteria on the first floor of Building No 3 and drinking some cold bottled milk in one gulp, Egashima goes to the library. The four-story library, its walls decorated with chocolate-coloured tiles, stands out from the other buildings when it gets dark as the windows of the reading rooms are illuminated by modern light fixtures. The reading room on the second floor is stocked with a variety of newspapers, pamphlets, booklets, and magazines. Egashima looks at the front page of one newspaper, flips it over, and moves on to the next. There's nothing about the recent earthquake in any of the newspapers. Relief measures had lasted for two weeks, and Egashima's unit had then returned to camp with the other teams. Egashima knew that he would not be on time for the first-period class, and he arrived at the university shortly before the lecture ended. He was very determined to come to class that day because the lecture on Literature was scheduled to be held.

About a dozen students were quietly studying in the reading room. Egashima asked a member of the staff about entering the reference room behind it. After being informed that it was fine to go in there, he gratefully entered the room.

He stood in front of the complete collection of Natsume Soseki's works displayed on retractable racks. Lined up neatly without any gaps, the books silently dominated the shelves. For a moment, Egashima thought he was looking at an exorbitantly expensive product.

Egashima looked at his watch. There was still some time left before the second-period lecture would start. He glanced over at the shelves again. There were different patterns and colours on the various book spines, and there were more than twenty volumes in total. He would like to pull one out and leaf through

it but refrained from doing so lest the complete collection might be disturbed. The thought occurred to him that he had never before looked at a book collection such as the one in front of him now. This realization soon led him to other different thoughts of one kind or another.

Egashima returned to the reading room entrance. Many students had finished their first class and were standing around there, and Egashima mingled with them. It was the first time in two weeks that Egashima really felt that he was indeed a university student. It was a nice feeling, too.

Egashima entered Lecture Hall 333 through a door at the rear. At the same time, a group of three or four students came in from the front. The girl who had helped him to read the difficult kanji in the second lesson was among them. Moving further into the lecture room, Egashima saw that his female senior was already seated in her usual place. Their eyes met. She raised her right hand slightly and signalled a casual acknowledgement using the palm of her hand. Then with the back of her hand and fingers, she urged her junior to go up to the front, which Egashima did. This time, however, he sat in the corner seat to the left of the aisle, two rows behind where he had sat during the second lecture. It was strangely comfortable to sit there, but somehow Egashima also felt like he had forfeited something.

<After saying goodbye, Sanshiro left the room. When he came to the main hallway, at its far end was the young lady he had encountered at the pond. She was standing in the square of light, tinted with the green from outside that fell through the entryway glass. Startled to see her, Sanshirō lost the rhythm in his gait. The silhouette of the young lady painted darkly on a floating canvas of air, took a step forward. Sanshirō moved forward too as if being beckoned. The two figures approached each other, destined to pass within the confines of the corridor.>

"They'll meet!" Professor Kamachi interjected.

< *As the woman ..... she suddenly lifted her gaze and looked straight at the man. Her soft eyes..... under contoured lids. Her prominent black eyelashes brought them to life.*>

"Soseki's depiction of this woman – How would you describe her? Is she a ravishing beauty, or merely beautiful? What is a beautiful feminine body? And how feminine can a beautiful body be?"

Today, as usual, Professor Kamachi's good-natured bantering enlivened the classroom. The laughter of the few male students attending the lecture rang louder than that of the women. Egashima also was slightly amused. He suddenly thought of his female senior seated a few rows behind him, and the image of her that arose in his mind caused a suppressed laugh.

<*The young lady proceeded on her way. Sanshirō stayed where he was and kept watching the woman's back. When .... she looked back. Sanshirō felt himself panic, and his cheeks flushed red. .... She turned to the right and disappeared behind the white walls.*>

"The central theme of this novel starts from here, but several pages will overlap until the two of them meet again."

<*Sanshirō's spirit grew restless. When he attended lectures, they sounded distant..........*

By and by, autumn reached its peak. Sanshirō's appetite increased. The season had arrived in which no 23-year-old young man could .... Sanshirō knew three worlds. One was far away..........It smells like before the 15th year of Meiji. All in this world was peaceful and still, but it was only half awake..........

In the second world, there was.........and the steady breathing of a pure and serene air ....The third world was dazzling and vibrant like springtime........

Finally, to crown it all, there were beautiful women......... There were lots of beautiful women. Beautiful women could be translated in many ways.>

"In this story, Tokyo and the Meiji era are described in Sanshiro's words, but they are representative of Soseki's thinking. As a sense of femininity is also woven into the fabric of the story, Sanshiro's daily actions and thoughts are naturally imbued with his feelings regarding women. He says he is usually relaxed in their presence although at times he also feels nervous."

<.... The garden gate suddenly opened. To his surprise, the young lady from the pond appeared in the garden.......The moment Sanshirō saw the woman framed off by this narrow space he suddenly had an insight......."Flowers are best when cut and viewed in a vase." The woman bowed as she addressed him with these initial words. While bowing, she gazed at Sanshirō.>

"Well, the story develops further from here. However, I'm sorry to disappoint you, but I would like to end today's lecture here. I have an urgent matter to attend to. I know it is thirty minutes early. Please look forward to the next lecture." As he said these words, Professor Kamachi stepped out of the room.

Although he knew he would have to miss the first-period class that evening, nevertheless Egashima was eager to come to the university because he wanted to attend the lecture on Literature. Ironically, the lecture now ends in only one hour. His female senior says that she will go to the library as she intends to take her regular bus home. Egashima wavers but then states that he's going straight to the bus stop. He had been to the library only an hour ago. From the third floor, he descends to the second floor, walks across the corridor lit by two mercury-vapour lamps and from there descends to the first and into the lobby. His colleagues and the other students still have half an hour to go before their lecture is due to end, so the place is empty. Although Egashima feels a little tired, he decides to walk as far as the second bus stop from the entrance to the university. It

will be nice to walk alone for a change, looking up at the night sky and holding a paperback in his hand. He takes a quick look at the notice board and leaves the lobby. From the tree-lined street, most of the small windows in several of the dormitories for civil servants at the back of the university are lit up. It is still too early to go to bed. Businesses are still open also.

For Egashima who works and sleeps with an all-male squad that is strict about punctuality, it is easy at times to feel that his life is somewhat tied down. On occasions like tonight, though, the faint lights and signs of family life remind him of a familiar and friendly village.

After exiting the tree-lined road, Egashima, instead of crossing over the pedestrian bridge, turned right immediately and continued to walk alone.

The cool night breeze soothes his tired body. It's a quiet time and feels almost as if he is being released from the intense hustle and bustle of his daytime job. As he walks along, it's not overly hushed, the streets are moderately lit, and some people, though sparse, are still coming and going. Such is the atmosphere in the environs of the university around 9 p.m.

At the first big intersection, the pedestrian signal begins to flash causing Egashima to jog over to the other side. Looking back, he sees a few cars waiting behind the stop lines on either side of the road as they prepare to move the moment the traffic light changes to green. On the corner of the sidewalk, Egashima notices a coffee shop. It's brighter than the surrounding ones with its name displayed on an electrical fitting above the entrance which also served as a decorative sign inviting customers inside the glass door.

As he walks further along, Egashima sees a girl walking in front of him. She's the student who helped him with the difficult kanji. Egashima lengthens his stride and after four or five paces catches up with her. Nodding a brief greeting, he begins to speak.

"Thank you for the other day."

The girl stops and looks at Egashima. For the moment, she seems perplexed and makes no response. She has a somewhat surprised and quizzical

expression on her face as if to say "Eh? What's this about?" However, almost immediately she becomes calmer and simply stands there gazing at Egashima.

"Thank you for helping me, - uh, *Sanshiro,* in the Literature class," Egashima explained.

"Augh, that," she merely replies with a slight smile on her face. The voice tone implies that, for her, what she did wasn't a big deal.

However, Egashima is glad that he has finally conveyed his sense of gratitude to this girl. Her reaction is tacit confirmation that she too remembers the incident. Egashima felt happy about that as well.

After that, Egashima doesn't say any more about the matter.

"Do you always walk home?"

"No, class finished early tonight so I took this road home with my friend for the first time. She has just returned to the university as she forgot something. Normally I take the regular bus from the university and go straight home:"

"My class finished early, too, and I thought that it would simply be nice to walk for a while looking at the stars."

"That's cool!"

"By the way, you walk fast. It's as if your legs are longer!"

"Excuse me, but that's my usual way of walking even though these shoes make it hard to do so."

"Where do you work during the day?"

"I'm a clerk at a hospital."

"And you commute from home?"

"No, I lodge at a boarding house and go from there."

"I do this - bang, bang," Egashima says as he makes a motion as if shooting a gun and then feels a little embarrassed.

"Is that so? But you don't look like a soldier at all. Training must be tough."

"Ah, there's not that not much to it when you get used to it."

After talking about work, their conversation just moved on naturally to

other things. They walked to the next bus stop and continued past it to the next and the next. Even if the bus he would normally take happened to pass by, Egashima didn't take any notice of it. He just continued walking. The girl and himself must have walked for over 30 minutes. Even so, Egashima felt that the distance and time were considerably shorter.

After crossing a bridge that was poorly lit, turning left, and going down a gentle downhill slope, they came to the tracks with the fitting points for the streetcar. Here, there is a little more gathering of people than on the quiet road they had just taken. Still, compared to the bustle in the evenings, the place was pretty quiet. The insides of buses and streetcar carriages stood out in the darkness due to the bright interior lighting of the vehicles. Most of the trams are still carrying people going home after their day's activities but normally at this time of night, the number of passengers standing is rather small. For Egashima, this was not a normal night. It had become something new and completely different.

Near the stop for transferring to the bus going to the camp the girl said "My place is near here, so I won't take the bus." Egashima was taken aback. She continued walking in the direction where the transfer bus makes a turn. After parting, Egashima walked the short distance to the usual Yakuencho bus stop. Waiting there, he realized that the girl and himself went home in the same direction. He was also aware that for some strange reason, he hadn't even asked her name.

The billboards with movie titles on top of the wall across the road were lit by the lights of cars turning in that direction. Egashima gazed wryly at the title of one of the movies. It read, *"The Youngsters."*

6

aargh, splash, squish, zaah

The inside of Egashima's army boots is soaked from the torrential rain. Thick black mud sticks to their outsides making movement ponderous. Most of the surrounding area is covered in sludge and difficult to walk. It's a desperate struggle to try and prevent one's legs from getting mired down or from slipping. The camouflage trousers feel like fatigues made of heavy clay. His mackintosh has not prevented any part of his body from getting wet, and now the heavy trench coat seems only to add to an increase in sweat.

As the response team continued to struggle in these precarious conditions, darkness began to fade with the dawn. Gradually, the contours of the devastated area became a little clearer. However, as the rain continued to fall, it also becomes obvious that the precipitation peak remains to be reached. So, the temporary facilities and equipment they brought for emergency measures need to be covered and protected from the rain.

As a member of the joint response team, Egashima entered the disaster area the night before. They were assigned the task of setting up a temporary communication station. This would take a few hours. Everything had to be done in the dark. At long last, it seemed that the mission is just about completed.

The squad leader starts grumbling once again, and though his voice is low so as not to be overheard by others, the message is forceful and sharp.

"Hey, don't be so damn sluggish, Egashima - if you slack off we won't make it on time, and the sun is already up."

"Aye, you're right there. I'll go and cut some of that overgrown grass on the ridge below us."

"And stop that goddamn grass from making those rustling sounds!"
"Got it."

The rain stopped and gradually it turned into a lovely morning, with

mountains in the distance visible through the gaps in the clouds. The area seemed to be veiled in morning mists. It's impossible to determine where the old mobile communication shelters, antennas, and other equipment are buried. The whole place is just a silent forest. Several species of birds twitter and sing. Their sounds resonate as if amplified. Egashima's wet and sweaty body seems like a frozen grass doll that must nevertheless continue to keep moving. However, there's some satisfaction in having completed a huge job in one night, and he feels that nature is on his side. Means of radio communications have been set up and were working as they were intended to. Growing morning light now shone through the bushes. He allowed himself a breather.

As he rested, a bird which looked like a white sparrow, flew down, perched on his dirty hand, and started to chirp. "Cute!" Egashima thought. Just like someone pretty he had once met, like a girl he had walked with….

His reverie was suddenly disturbed by a voice shouting, "Hey, we're still in a tight spot here, don't let your guard down!" Startled, Egashima, fatigued and chilled to the bone, realized that he had dozed off for a moment.

For the first time in five days, Egashima heads down the tree-lined slope from the camp to get on the bus. It was raining, but Egashima's feelings were if anything softened by the drizzle. He knows that today, he is going to be late for the first-period lecture yet once again. His two colleagues probably have already arrived at the university. Not having to share the bus ride with them might even be a good thing. On occasions, he prefers to be left alone, in his own world. With such thoughts crossing his mind, he continues to walk on.

There are lots of passengers on the bus on rainy days. The heat from their bodies mingled with wet umbrellas makes the air inside the bus humid, fogging up the windows and making it difficult to see the outside. It is the same on every bus.

The stop for the transfer bus was crowded with people holding open umbrellas. The road too was congested with slow-moving cars. Trams announce

their approach and sound their horns more often than on fine days. Egashima, who is resigned to being late for class, feels in no rush. After folding their umbrella, people move quickly. They are in a hurry to get out of the rain and on the bus. They show scant regard for others. Egashima boards the bus.

As usual, Egashima goes to grab a hanging strap near the exit. There is an empty seat just to his left. Egashima normally doesn't sit down unless there are very few passengers, and today he also decided to let another passenger have the seat. However, the passenger standing next to him doesn't seem to be all that interested in sitting down. She looks at Egashima and makes a slight bow. Egashima is taken aback, blinks his eyes in surprise, and instinctively nods in return. He smiles when he sees her cheerful face, her cheeks slightly reddened. Egashima gestures with his chin a few times urging the girl to sit on the vacant seat. Though appearing slightly hesitant, she does so. Egashima has again met the familiar female student, this time on a crowded bus.

Egashima hasn't yet spoken to the girl and feels he shouldn't talk from a standing position to someone who is sitting. The girl has a bag on her lap. She had taken the small satchel containing Egashima's history textbook and paperback off his shoulder as she went to sit down. So Egashima is left carrying nothing but his umbrella. His body felt lighter.

The exterior is invisible through the fogged-up windows of the bus, and the female student is sitting with her eyes fixed on the backrest of the seat in front of her. The bus has to pass through two large intersections to reach the university. There is a pedestrian crossing about halfway between these intersections, but even though it's a rainy day and the bus is moving slower than usual, they will arrive at the university bus stop very shortly. The first intersection traffic light is green, and the bus goes through quickly. The large windshield wipers keep moving back and forth. Then they come to the bridge.

Egashima switches the hanging strap onto his left hand. With his right hand, he pats the female student's shoulder lightly and writes 'n-a-m-e' in small letters with his index finger on the cloudy window beside her. The female student

looks at the word and pauses for a moment. Then with her index finger, writes 'a- i- u- e' and immediately erases the letters with her middle finger. With a nod, Egashima puts down 'e-ga-shi-ma'. The girl nods, smiles again, and then erases what he has written. The fog on the window disappears where she has wiped, and it's only there that the streetscape appears to run alongside the bus. The girl turns her head and keeps looking out the window.

The bus arrives in front of the university. The standing passengers get off first, so Egashima and the girl are separated. When she alights, he takes his small bag from her.

"Thank you. What's your first class?"

"Economics."

On hearing this, Egashima leaves and sets out for Building No 3. Only twenty minutes have elapsed since the beginning of his first-period lecture, so he goes straight to Lecture Hall 324 on the second floor.

After taking his seat, Egashima casually opens the history textbook and then looks at the class timetable inserted into his notebook. He notes that classes in Economics are held in Lecture Hall 332 in Building No 3, the same building in which he is now attending class.

After the first class, as Egashima is moving up to the third floor, his female senior is also about to climb the stairs.

"   "Egashima, you had to work hard for the first time in a long while. It must have been difficult in the Beppu Mountains with all that heavy rain."

"I only got back this afternoon."

"You could have taken a rest for today."

"I suppose so, but I wanted to meet *Bijin-senpai*, so I came to class."

"Oh, it's so nice of you to say that."

"I guess you just took Business Administration in Lecture Hall 325?"

"That's right. Why are you asking me?"

"No, uh- it's only that…"

The short ten-minute break between lectures is a precious time. Lecture

Hall 333 has many groups of friends chatting with each other. Women's laughter in particular makes for a lively atmosphere. Egashima forgets his tiredness from having worked hard all day when talking to other students in this classroom. During the class on Literature, he finds he can focus more intently on what the teacher writes on the blackboard and also on the brief summaries he writes in his textbook than in the other lecture rooms.

"*Bijin-senpai,* this classroom is always beautiful and bright."

"Ah, you men. Can't you bring up another topic, such as love!"

"Gyao - Oow!"

"A joke, joke! Hurry along, and move up there to the front. "

Driven away, Egashima takes what he considers to be a passive and safe seat, the same one he had sat in the previous week.

Prof. Kamachi is commenting on the text.

"Sanshiro says that his current life is becoming more meaningful than it had been in Kumamoto. This feeling seems to deepen as each day goes by. Of the three worlds he once thought about, his life at present is truly that of the second and the third world."

Today, the professor is also selecting students to read aloud.

"The next scene is very interesting and important to the plot. It's about what happened to Sanshirō when he went to see a chrysanthemum doll exhibition that was very crowded. The scene shows the connection between the two main characters, as well as their reactions – physical and verbal. Let's have a female read it."

Egashima recalls the name on the fogged window glass. He had made a note of the letters on his class timetable. What might the kanji be? Of course, it would have to be her surname.

< *Mineko turned forward again and was swept along by the crowd toward the exit. Sanshirō pushes his way through the crowd......... Mineko began moving through the swell of sightseers. Sanshirō, of course, accompanied her.*

Half a block on, she stopped amid the crowd.

"Where are we?

Sanshirō…………………………..

"Can you walk another block or so?" he asked her.

"Yes, let's go.

The two of them crossed the stone bridge…………………..upstream by the water's edge. They were out in the open now, away from the crowd.

"Beautiful!" As she spoke, Mineko sat down on the grass.

Sanshirō, too,…………..on the grass.

"………………………………….."

"Are you feeling better now? If you're better, then shall we head back?

"Lost children."

She looked at him and repeated these words. Sanshirō didn't respond.

"Do you know another English term for 'lost children?'"

The question caught Sanshirō by surprise, and he couldn't say whether he knew or not.

"Would you like me to tell you?"

"Please."

"It's 'stray sheep' -- Do you know what I mean?

He felt he understood what "stray sheep" meant. At the same time, he didn't seem to understand……………… Mineko suddenly grew serious. "

"Do I come across as cheeky?"

Sanshirō sensed a sense of exculpation in her attitude………..She seemed bitter. Mineko said abruptly, "We should be going." The two of them set off. When Sanshirō was about to say something, there was mud in front of his feet………..in the middle of which was placed a handy stone for a foothold. Sanshirō jumped across without touching the stone support. Then he looked back at Mineko. Mineko had planted her right foot on top of the stone and stood.

………………………. Sanshirō held out his hand from his side.

"Hold it."

"No, I'm fine," she said with a smile. While his hand was held out, she recovered her balance but remained on the stone. Sanshirō withdrew his hand. Mineko shifted her weight to her right foot and leaped deftly over the puddle onto her left. Determined to clear the mud, she jumped too hard and stumbled forward from the excess momentum. She stopped herself with both hands against Sanshirō's arms. "Stray sheep," she whispered again to herself. She was so near that Sanshirō could feel her breath

The professor tells the student to stop reading there.

"Thank you for your beautiful diction. I have somehow forgotten how many pages you read. Everyone was enchanted, and Soseki too was delighted. Stray sheep, and lost children. I wonder what the great author himself would say if he were here now and talking about the ladies or the men who are in this class......."

The light laughter of some of the surrounding women echoed through to Egashima's ears.

The professor continues to explain.

"The next time Sanshiro and Mineko will meet is on a sports day at an athletic meeting in Ikebata. Until that episode, I will proceed by talking about the drinking of *akazake* and eating raw horse meat, as well as other barbarous forms of lifestyles native to Kumamoto. Soseki also drank the *akazake* red alcohol. So, I feel a close affinity with him. The spirit of students in the Meiji era is also interesting in that they pursued various types of ideals. So, what was Soseki like when he was a student?"

While listening to the professor speak, Egashima thinks again about the letters "*a, i, u, e*" which the girl had written on the fogged-up window of the bus. Could it be *"a, i, ko, i?"* No, that didn't seem right. If written using these two kanji, her surname would then be "Love - Love."

< Sanshiro was fresh in from the country and just starting his university studies. He had no significant scholarship to his name, and his personal views were still evolving. There was no reason for Mineko to respect him like…………………. Now that he thought about it, perhaps she took him for a fool. Earlier, when ……….>

The professor begins to comment again.

"Soseki fell in love, too. Sanshiro, being a country boy and naive, was a bit slow to catch on to city life and its women. But Soseki, on the other hand, was born and grew up in Tokyo, so that wouldn't have happened to him here in Kumamoto. It is said this story is modelled on his student Sanshiro."

Listening to the professor, Egashima thinks about his own circumstances and background. If Tokyo is the capital and Kumamoto is a city, what about the place where he himself was born and raised? 'I come from there and now I'm here.' Egashima reminds himself that Kumamoto is a city and he has gone there from a small rural town. That makes him the same as the main character of the story they are reading. However, unlike the hero in *Sanshiro*, Egashima regards himself as an undeveloped person. If he were to become the hero of a literary story, then that tale would be a low-level one. Just being here in the city of Kumamoto is enough. There's no need to seek fame or heroism.

Egashima is glad that he understands the novel they're studying in the Literature class.

At the end of class, Egashima is thinking about something wholly unrelated to the study of Literature. Then he completely forgets what is going through his mind when he sees his female senior talking animatedly with another student as they leave the classroom. Egashima is experiencing all kinds of weird surging going through his body.

"*Biji-senpai*, let's walk to the bus stop together while chatting."

"What on earth has come over you at this stage?"

"Today, I want to hear about your theory of literature."

"Hahaha, the lecture left a strong impression on you. Egashima, Literature is born from the conflict between reason and emotion."

"*Sanshiro* is a warm, dream story, isn't it?"

"Egashima, yours is a natural emotion, very normal because you are a normal person. Normal – normal!"

What his senior said sounded interesting in an odd way.

It was no longer raining but the way out seemed to be shrouded in fog. Oyama comes chasing after them, swinging his folded umbrella like a baseball bat.

"Big Senior, Egashima-senpai, this is Oemachi Town and we are here and not in foggy London."

"I bet Egashima can't compose haiku in the style of Soseki."

"*Bijin-senpai,* I was absent from the lecture on 'Soseki and Haiku,' so I don't know his style."

"Come on! All you have to do is make a poem of five, seven, and five syllables. Like this:

> *Night fog*
>
> *Street lights*
>
> *Just like London*

Isn't that a great haiku?"

"Just what you'd expect! Let me compose a haiku

> *Changed to*
>
> *A foggy university*
>
> *In London*

Good, don't you think?"

"I don't study literature like my two seniors, but I'll try one;

> *Covered in fog*
>
> *Two talk well*
>
> *About Soseki*

Am I a good haiku poet?

"What's it with the three of us? We're all on about fog. I don't even know if the correct term is fog or haze or mist, and I wonder if these are seasonal words. But fog will do. Joining my two juniors has somehow given birth to a great haiku!"

"Talking about Soseki is nice, but let's go out drinking together sometime. Being a carpenter, I'm usually free when it's raining."

"Free time? We can only go out on Sunday. Isn't that right Egashima?"

"   "*Bijin-senpai*, I can't go out this Sunday. I'm on duty."

"Oh, I forgot. Sunday is sentry day for you. Ah, poor Egashima! OK then. Tomorrow is Saturday. You know that the second-period class for both of you is cancelled tomorrow. You will be free after the first class. I'll skip my second class. So, let's go downtown tomorrow night."

The matter was settled in the middle of the dimly lit tree-lined avenue. In the haze, only the area near the main exit gate was visible, as if it were the mouth of a round tunnel leading out from a mountain covered with dense fog.

7

dō—dō—, dō—su—, thunk, dōh—su

After freely practicing the various basic techniques of footwork, strikes, and thrusts, Egashima's body had loosened up a great deal, but the heat and humidity had made him sweaty.

"Put on your mask," the instructor ordered.

The mask interferes with and disrupts Egashima's breathing.

"Start! Practice freely with an opponent."

Trying to master different strikes and follow through demands good form, agile footwork, and much-repeated effort.

"Move around more! Strike! Don't let up your spirit!"

The trainees change opponents. Egashima's lower-ranking subordinates, such as Private Matsushita, who is just a beginner, are all taller than him.

"The first *Ippon*! Restart!"

Duelers move speedily and slam into each other with a stamp of the front foot. Egashima's left wrist is struck by his opponent and the arm goes numb.

"You lack fighting spirit. Strikes don't have enough force. Practice!"

The tip of the opponent's wooden bayonet hits Egashima's chin, causing severe pain.

"Everyone's *kiai* is too weak. Raise your voices. Shout, *kiai, kiai*! Once more, thrust faster! Faster!"

As the number of repeated practice bouts increases, Egashima's mental and physical condition improves and he is able to listen to Nakano's instructions with greater acceptance. Gradually his rhythm and sharpness are refined also.

"*Yame!* Stop! Remove your masks and take a short rest. The remaining bouts will begin immediately after the break. Be ready to compete right away."

Egashima takes off his mask and removes the shoulder pads and breast protector. He is usually surprised at how light his body felt after practicing. When

training is finished and on leaving the gymnasium, he always relishes the feel of the air's sweetness outside. For now, that will have to wait though.

"Rest is over. Get ready to start the unfinished bouts. Get into position. There will be special intensive practice from now till the end. Start!"

"Strike, move, thrust!" Instructor Nakano shouts over and over.

Egashima's agility and sharpness gradually become conspicuous among the contestants.

In martial arts exercises, where quick decisions and reactions make all the difference, there is simply no time allowed for the lack of concentration.

The shadows of the sago palms reflected in the small garden are created by the lights that illuminate Building No. 1 and Building No. 4. The greenness of the beautifully manicured garden lawn stands out in contrast. The Evening Division, which has about 1,200 students taking two lectures a night, creates a very different atmosphere from that experienced by those taking daytime courses.

Egashima and Oyama finish the first period five minutes early, so they decide to wait for their senior in the lobby.

Students who have had the next class cancelled hurry through the lobby one after another on the way out.

"Do you think she will really skip the second period?"

"Oyama, *Bijin-senpai* doesn't lie. Her face may appear to say different but she has a beautiful heart. That's what I mean when I call her 'Beautiful Senior.'"

"Egashima-senpai, I'm looking forward to going drinking with you both."

Shortly after they started talking, the female senior appears, giving her usual salute and with a smile on her face. Oyama, with a serious expression, mumbles something to his senior about overdoing things by skipping her second class. However, his soft-spoken voice indicates that what he has just said was not in admonition but rather out of sheer delight.

In front of the main gate, the female senior hails a passing taxi and it doesn't take long to reach the downtown area. They get out of the taxi at Torichosuji and the three of them start walking down the main shopping street of Shimatori. It's a rather busy Saturday night downtown, and coming here straight from the university leaves Egashima and Oyama's heads reeling for a few moments. They find it difficult to focus properly. It seems as if they have suddenly landed in an unusually gorgeous locality. The two of them just continue to follow their senior as she leads the way.

The front part of the main street has a roof and this section is called Shinchigai - "new urban territory." The senior explains to her two juniors that, sometime in the near future, the entire Shimotori Street would become a pedestrian-only arcade just like the rival upper street of Kamitori on the other side of the tram tracks.

"We're there."

They go into a nice little restaurant. Egashima and Oyama sit side by side on the tatami at a rectangular table while their senior sits on her own across from them. After talking to the proprietress of the restaurant for a few moments, the senior didn't ask the two of them what they wanted to eat but had a waitress immediately bring three glasses of draft beer.

"Guys, until what time are you free?"

"On Saturdays, lights go out at 11:00 at the barracks, which is an hour later than usual."

"How about you, Oyama?"

"The last JNR train is at... er...."

"It's 8:30 now, so until 10 o'clock is fine for both of you then."

"Yes," both Egashima and Oyama answered in unison.

The three of them raise and clink glasses full of beer. "*Kampai!*"

"The name of this restaurant is Shigure. The manager is an acquaintance of mine. I've ordered a set of local cuisine, so we'll get a lot of delicious food. Eat as much as you like. The first serving is *basashi,* horsemeat

sashimi."

Egashima had been feeling exhausted following his earlier martial arts practice but now he's very relaxed and grateful.

"*Bijin-senpai:* today has been a full day for me - work, study, and now play."

"Me too. It didn't rain, so I was able to make good progress with my outdoor work," Oyama reports with a slight grin.

The female senior is really pleased with the expression of contentment on the two men's faces. Low-volume familiar music is playing in the background. "I like this song. It's *'Queen of Sheba'* by Raymond Lefevre, and the one before it was also good.. Do you know who sang *'Both Sides Now,'* Egashima?"

"Judith Collins," Egashima replies at once.

"Correct, and *'Those were the Days'* is sung by?"

"Mary Hopkins."

They reminisce about their favourite songs and pieces of music.

"They are all lovely songs and that other one, oh yes *'White Lovers'* by Francis Lai is also really nice. You know it's the theme song for the Grenoble Winter Olympics in Claude Lelouch's film."

'The Three Bells' by the Browns is really beautiful. So, too, was Billy Vaughn Orchestra's rendition of the *'Pearly Shells'* and *'Covered Wagon.'* These and Percy Faith Orchestra's version of *'A Summer Place'* are among my all-time favourites," *Bijin-senpai* declared.

"Oh, I remember *"Natsu no Hino no Koi'.* It was the theme song for the radio program "Good evening, Gojo desu." One of my favourites was that song, which is about falling in love in the summer."

"Egashima, I think you probably also used to listen to the broadcast from the coffee shop's satellite studio. How about Oyama? What songs do like to listen to?"

"Oh, I'm not….."

"Really? But you used to listen to…"

"I'm not so fond of the oldies."

"Oh, I'm sorry. I also like modern folk songs by The Brothers Four, the Kingston Trio, Joan Baez, and so on. Egashima, you like Mitch Miller don't you? His *'River Kwai March'* and other marching songs are unforgettable. I used to watch the "Sing Along with Mitch" show on TV. That's why I know about him."

"*Bijin-senpai,* you know so much. I'm always impressed."

"How about movies?"

"I like movies too. I especially liked '*The Sound of Music*', which was screened in 70mm format. I saw it in the autumn of my last year in high school. I took the express bus to Kumamoto just to go and see it. There were so many people there that night that I couldn't even sit down and had to watch the entire film standing up. I found the beautiful scenery especially moving as I think most of the audience did as well."

"I watched it too, of course, and enjoyed it but overall, I think I preferred the songs and dances of *'West Side Story.'*"

"I like Westerns, too. The sunset over Monument Valley from John Ford's *'She Wore a Yellow Ribbon'* is a truly beautiful scene. I saw it when I was little and again when in high school. The music in it was also great."

"Egashima, do you know what a 'yellow ribbon' means?"

"Of course, I do. It means that, ah, …It's a declaration of intent."

"Yes, that's it. By the way, I've come to the conclusion that we Japanese are obsessed with the West, especially America. Well, Japan was rather poor after the war. I suppose seeing the rich and bright life of America from an early age left its mark on us. Oyama, what do you like?"

"I like Japanese pop songs. Things like *'Blue Light Yokohama'*"

"Ah, Ayumi Ishida. She's probably about the same age as you guys."

"She's the same age as Egashima-senpai."

"Oyama, you're two years younger then. There are just so many of you baby boomers."

"Egashima-senpai belongs to the first group, those born between 1947

and 1948."

"If I'd gone straight to college, I'd be in the fourth year now. How many of our age do you think are in college? I read in the newspaper that there are 16% or 17% when university and junior college enrollments are combined. The number of lower graders has increased slightly, but not that much. Only the elite went directly to college."

"Are we in the Evening Division included in the number you just mentioned?" Egashima wants to know.

"I don't know. Probably not. But consider yourselves lucky to be studying at university."

Two or three groups of customers have come and gone while they were chatting. They had only drunk a few beers but the senior's face was already turning red. Suddenly, the content of the conversation took a completely different twist.

"Let's talk about literature. Come on, pour it, pour it... nourish your soul with literature!"

Her voice becomes louder as she continues.

"You know, *Kusamakura*. I read it when I was in high school. You've probably been to Oama Town, too. It's in a mountainous area with mandarin orange groves. The novel is set there. You've probably heard these phrases: *"Approach everything rationally, and you become harsh. Pole along in the stream of emotions, and you will be swept away by the current. Give free rein to your desires, and you become uncomfortably confined."*

Oyama shook his head and asked Egashima, "This *Ku-sa-ma-ku-ra*, is she referring to a 'pillow made of grass'?"

Egashima laughed loudly and haughtily responded, "Oyama, let me tell you something. *Kusamakura* is the title of one of Natsume Soseki's novels. *'Approach everything rationally, and you become harsh'* is a line in the opening paragraph."

Egashima had spoken as if he was very familiar with the novel.

His female senior sarcastically said, "Egashima, you study literature. So, naturally, you know more than Oyama, which makes you more distinguished."

On hearing this, Oyama retorts "I wonder if studying literature makes Egashima-senpai more distinguished than I," and with what seems to be a dissatisfied look on his face he gulps down more beer.

After a brief lull, their senior adds.

"I wouldn't blame you guys for disliking me. Seems I'm always preaching at you. Right?"

She then goes on to say that she feels keenly the close connection between university lectures and her work, especially when she is working at her uncle's judicial scrivener's office. She explains why and stresses that studying is very important. Egashima and Oyama listen attentively to what she has to say.

The senior continues on.

"These days, there are a lot of student protests in universities. It's so ironic. Students study hard in high school to get into college. Then they spend their time demonstrating. What an absolute waste! Their parents must be mortified. I'm really at a loss to understand just what the protesters are complaining about. Society is full of absurdities. Things don't always go according to plan or measure up to one's expectations. That's how it's always been. I feel like there's a difference between fairness and true justice within organizations and even society in general. But throwing stones or waving sticks will not solve things. It's not even bravery. If you have courage, don't cover your face with a towel. It's a cowardly thing to do. Meanwhile, other students are taking things seriously and attending classes. On the other hand, I want students to pursue their ideals and justice more and more. Is my thinking due to my individualism?"

"Yeah," the two guys reply as one, casting a quick look at each other and hiding the grins on their faces.

The senior continues on a more personal note.

"Egashima, do you go back to your hometown often?"

"No, not really. I haven't been back there since New Year's."

"You should go home more often. Just showing up makes parents happy. That's what filial piety is all about. You don't live that far from our hometown. It's not as if you have to keep in contact by writing a letter."

"No," Egashima agreed.

"However, people often say that you can't fully understand a parent's feelings until you become a parent yourself. It is also said that the good things about being young cannot be understood until you become old."

Empty platters and small dishes are piled up on the table. The two men had eaten to their heart's content. Their heads too are also full. The senior picks up the bill and pays it. Then they leave the restaurant.

The main street is still bustling with revellers as the three of them part ways on Torichosuji, where they had gotten out of the taxi earlier. One heads back to live with relatives, another to a place where bugles announced bedtime, and the third returns to a house where saws and planes are lined up.

8

baa-za, thump, pound, ga-zza,

"Have you finished digging?"

"Yes. And the covers for the networks are nearly completed."

"Good. I'll start checking the ones that are ready. If there are any flaws, the team is responsible and will need to fix them without taking a break."

The onset of terrible heat after the end of the rainy season is sudden and scorching hot, and the human body needs time to adapt to it. High temperatures coupled with the suffocating humidity add greater discomfort to the hardship of working under the sun. Furthermore, the drills for erecting the antenna poles are conducted while wearing uniforms made for carrying the equipment. Egashima's unit had to struggle with soil that was not yet fully dry. He felt like a miner who had to work in a deep and heat-filled coal pit.

At last, the day's exercises and drills are over. But then the supervisor starts to give out further instructions.

"It was a perfect day for performing today's drills. Now we're going to jog back to base. Every squad member should run without breaking rank. If you're not feeling well, say so right now. Make sure to put the picks and pickaxes on the truck."

A few minutes later he announces, "No one wants to go in the vehicle, so everyone will run. I'm not aiming for speed. The goal is to finish. If someone gets sick, you can walk. But as you're all still young, I think you'll be fine. Do your best."

Egashima runs all the way back. After being dismissed, he rushes to the washroom and turns on the water tap. Tears of delight well up at tasting the coldness of the fresh underground water.

"Aah, ooh," he repeats with satisfaction while gulping it down.

"Hey, Egashima, don't leave the water running! Now we're going to

start cleaning the mud-stained floor. Everyone, gather into teams."

An evening breeze blows through the open window and it feels good. For the first time, Egashima sits in a window seat at the Literature lecture and feels half-satisfied. At the beginning of summer, the clothes students wear change completely from those worn in other seasons. When it gets hot, those who come directly to school from work are still wearing neckties. They simply remove the ties and put on short sleeves attire. In early summer a lecture room with lots of students naturally gets hot. The Literature class is nearly always full, but either because of the tension that students feel from the fact that they might be asked to read aloud or simply because the lectures are so enjoyable, creates an atmosphere in which they don't feel the heat as insufferable.

The professor begins by making remarks about a certain passage.

"We have looked at a few scenes since Mineko spoke of 'stray sheep.' We have seen how Sanshirō is often on edge and gets nervous. In their world, the one which we are now exploring, men, women, and young people often fret and squirm. One would think that people's worries seem wholly unnecessary due to the kind of world they lived in. Don't you think so, too? But I guess these kinds of contradictions are part of what makes a good novel."

<*There was still time until the evening.........Mineko and Sanshiro stepped out together.*

................It would be difficult for Sanshirō to create such an opportunity at will.

Sanshirō put it off for a long time........ While walking side by side,...>

"The rest of this chapter---, oh, I don't want you to read it. Aagh!"

The students burst into laughter at the professor's exaggerated performance and gestures. For those who had already read the novel in full and those now following the story along with the lecture, this scene adds

complications and tension to the narrative. Egashima is enjoying these developments and he laughs casually while looking around at the seats far behind him. He feels relieved to see his female senior also smiling. She is looking towards Egashima and furtively waves at him. Egashima returns her wave without hesitation.

As far as Egashima is concerned, every ninety minutes Literature lecture seems to last no longer than the blink of an eye. He believes this perception is due to the unique combination of several factors: the uproarious and quiet moments; laughter-filled instances and periods of enhanced stillness; and the common purpose that develops so naturally in the lecture room.

More than anything, probably the main reason the time passes so quickly is that the students are learning at the same time and for the same duration, and thus they are living in the present moment, an integrated here and now.

9

Tap, tap, tap, tap

On Sundays and national holidays, Egashima does shifts on guard duty. One afternoon, after finishing patrol he was about to enter the main barrack when he was called over by the guard commander.

"Leading Private Egashima, we have four visitors. Please accompany them to the flower bed area in front of headquarters. When they have finished sightseeing, come back here with them. This is a special order."

Egashima nervously replied, "Yes, I understand."

However, he was puzzled by the suppressed smile on the commander's face as he continued to explain the reason for giving the order.

"It's a perfect assignment for you, Egashima. This is a quiet camp, and the weather is fine today. I'm sure the visitors will be pleased with their guide."

The four visitors consist of three young children and a middle-aged woman who seems to be their mother. Egashima shows them around with due propriety and vigilance. They all seem to be happy and enjoying themselves a lot. When the woman said to Egashima "It must be very beautiful here when the azaleas are in full bloom," he replies politely, "Yes, that's right."

The woman continues.

"When I was eighteen, a person I loved left our hometown to join the National Police Reserve when it was just being established. I kept waiting a long time, but the person never returned. I detested the new Reserve Corps because it seemed as if the person I loved had been taken from me. In due course, I had an arranged marriage, and my three children have grown to what you see here. I am happy now but for some strange reason, I've always wanted to enter this camp even just once. Now that I'm allowed to see around this beautiful garrison, I can't help but recall those earlier days and my emotions are getting somewhat complicated."

Egashima straightens up on hearing the woman's story, and he is especially kind and even more attentive to their presence on the base. On their way out, when the woman tells Egashima "Today was a wonderful day" he is very pleased with the unexpected task that was given him that afternoon. He felt as if he had done a small favour that required very little commitment, but yet might bring long-lasting effects.

Egashima's sense of self-satisfaction remains until the next day's work shift and training drills.

<No matter how long Sanshirō would stand, he remained afraid, and the teacher would start talking. "………Let's talk of something more interesting."

"Please."

"I had a remarkable dream...... In it was a girl whom I'd only seen once before in my life. I suddenly met her again.

"It's a wonder you would know her."

``It's a dream. That's why I knew her. In a dream, one indulges the wondrous....

I told her she hadn't changed and when I asked her how she could remain unchanged, she answered back ...because her face of that year, her outfit of that month, and her hair of that day were the most to her liking.... When I told her that she was a picture at the time I met her, she replied that I was a poem at the time we met."

"What happened after that?" Sanshirō wanted to know.

"It happened. That's what's interesting.">

"The last chapter of this novel is approaching. At this stage, you men who are not confident about how you look, please tear up the book from the next page onwards. You women who have confidence in yourselves do the same. That means those of you who think you are beautiful."

The classroom erupts in laughter.

The first semester lectures are coming to an end and while they have concentrated on a single work by Soseki, the professor has enthralled the students by talking about literary topics related to the novel as well as life in the Meiji era. Summer vacation is about to start.

"That's enough about *Sanshiro*. Let's immerse ourselves in other works in the second semester," Prof. Kamachi announces and with that brings the lecture to a close.

Egashima had not developed the habit of sitting in the same section or seat for most of the first semester classes. He usually picked a seat depending on his mood that day. He never again sat in the seat from which he was asked to read aloud. As the semester progressed Egashima had tended to favour a seat by the window in the first row. It was only in the Literature class that he seemed to have a preferred place and seat in which to sit. He sometimes wondered why he had become so careful about all this. He thought it a little odd that he would even think about such things that really were matters of no particular significance.

After this lecture, Egashima stands up and shuffles toward the aisle. The female student who helped him read the kanji is already in the aisle. She glances at Egashima, smiles, and bows slightly. Egashima also lowers his head a little. The girl leaves the classroom, chatting with other students.

Today, Egashima misses the presence of his female senior. Although he doesn't remember exactly what it was, he can't forget that she had made some reference to the second-semester classes due to start in October the night the three of them went drinking together downtown on Shimatori Street. That was unusual as although she talked a lot about the past, she rarely had much to say about the future.

Leaving Lecture Room 333, Egashima looks sadly at the seat in the back row where the female senior always sat. He goes to the library, which was an unusual thing for him to do on his way home. However, he only peeked into the newspaper reading room and then continues down the stairs, passing through the meeting place lobby. There's no sign of his two colleagues or Oyama either.

For some reason, Egashima doesn't bother to read the few remaining pages of *Sanshirō,* even though he has no lectures for six weeks during summer vacation. Instead, he decides to read some of Soseki's earlier works. Despite being ridiculed by his superiors and subordinates for his studiousness, Egashima reads *"I Am a Cat"* and *"Botchan"* with assiduous attention. He finds these novels hilarious.

Egashima is intrigued by the name of a woman portrayed by Soseki as a mother figure in *"Botchan,"* a novel that was covered in a single lecture at university. The woman in *"Botchan"* is called Kiyo, the same name as Egashima's mother. She is popularly known as Kiyoko. The name "Kiyoko" also appears in Soseki's novel *"Light and Darkness."* Egashima remembers that his mother used to talk about Hanegi Bridge, a place that is mentioned in *"I am a Cat."* She often said that there was a suburban residence of the Hosokawa clan, in which her ancestors had served, located near the sleeve of that bridge.

Egashima didn't read any other novels by Soseki during the summer holidays. He didn't pick up another novel because he knew it would probably remain unfinished. There were a few times when he put off reading a novel so as to set aside some time for fun during the second-semester classes. At the same time, by having read several of Soseki's novels, Egashima felt like he had lost some of the diffidence he had previously lived with due to not having read such works. He also felt that his ability to think had improved. In bookstores, he noticed a growing curiosity for new books of all kinds, and he frequently would briefly browse through one or two.

Two interesting events happened to Egashima that summer.

One was at the Rural Youth Festival held in the Mt. Aso area. This is a large rally where young people who are engaged in farming both in Kyushu, and Okinawa, come together to exchange and enhance farming methods and form friendships. The slogan for the event that year was "Let's do our best to create a beautiful town or village." The average age of about 1,100 participants was twenty-two. Egashima went to the gathering as a member of a support team

engaged in erecting accommodation tents. This was his pretext for going, but he also just wanted to participate in the event as a fellow young man.

Sitting around the first night's bonfire and at the big campfire on the prairie the following night, Egashima was overwhelmed by the spirit and energy of this young farming group. When he ran into some acquaintances from the university, Egashima greeted them as if they were old friends. One of these opined "There's a lot of people of our generation here. They take real pride in their work in agriculture. Such thinking and attitude give me courage." "Farming can be a career filled with dreams and hopes," another said, adding that "A new culture will blossom in the environment they will create. Writers will come from there." A representative from a local agricultural Consultative Council espoused that "Many new stores will also open in towns. These will adopt new ways to prepare and sell agricultural products to customers." He emphasized that "This new culture will be passed on to the next generation, to their children and grandchildren." The overall consensus in all these discussions was that things should not be done haphazardly.

Another happening that deeply impressed Egashima that summer was the news of Apollo 11 and the first moon landing. This event illustrated the marvels of human potential and the importance of pursuing dreams. He had been very excited at the Tokyo Olympics when he was a sophomore in high school, but now he felt equally elated by the first moon landing. Areas such as radio wave propagation technology, communication technology, computer technology, and other engineering feats were all directly related to his work, and he was excited about their future development and the challenges this posed. The world was certainly moving forward and Egashima wanted to be part of that, to move with the flow. Such were the feelings and thoughts that permeated his mood in the summer of his twenty-first year.

Egashima couldn't wait for the day when the university classes would resume. Around that time, he also had a dream while he was asleep.

Egashima is sitting in his usual seat by the window in the classroom.

The side of the room consists of a single pane of glass. There are no dividing frames or beams. From the floor to the ceiling, from the front edge to the rear edge of the room, it's a wall of glass. Other classrooms are the same and all of them are connected in a large circle so that each classroom can be viewed from every other one. How many classrooms are there? Egashima is not sure. He has never counted them. At present all of them are full of students attending the lectures.

The large garden in the middle of the campus is full of greenery. Bright sunlight bathes the site. Benches have been placed in the shade and are available for student use during recess. Trees are reflected in the small stream which flows gently through the grounds. Grass and flowers sway in the breeze. Clouds float in the sky.

This dazzling scenery fades with the coming of night. The lantern tower which stands quietly in the garden lights up. The garden at night makes the view from the classroom even more enjoyable and soothes the mind. At night, the stars and moon are reflected in the stream.

Egashima is looking at a distant classroom facing him.

"Someone is looking at me," he thinks.

He kept watching. And watching. And watching.

The second-semester classes begin with the first-semester examinations. Egashima fails the Literature exam. He does well in other subjects but his result in Literature is a complete flop. One reason was the inability to sufficiently comprehend the text. Furthermore, his answers contained many incorrect kanji. Given his poor result here, Egashima realizes that he lacks basic language skills.

Exam results are posted on the notice board in the lobby. The examinees are listed in alphabetical order according to the Japanese syllabary, with no distinction between men and women. Scores for each course that the examinee had enrolled in are written on a standardized form. The name of each student and the high school they graduated from are also shown. Such a public airing of a

student's results is used as a means to stir them on to even greater academic efforts.   It's also easy to check how other students performed. So, with a slight qualm of conscience, Egashima searched for the letters *a, i. u, e.* and notices the name "Ai-Ue" listed in the table.

The leaves of the ginkgo trees have turned yellow, and fallen leaves begin to cover the tree-lined road on the campus. They do not form a complete carpet but at the same time, it is well-nigh impossible to avoid stepping on them when taking that road.

Autumn has fully set in and the development of academic courses is also quite advanced. While there were various liberal arts subjects such as foreign languages and history which a student could enroll in, quite a few seem to have opted for specialized courses such as economics and law, or subjects that directly relate to their work. Egashima's female senior said that those students were most likely employed in public institutions such as prefectural offices or City Hall.

Egashima is about to climb the stairs to go to Lecture Room 121 in Building No. 1 when he spots the female senior in the hallway on the first floor. He would like to talk to her, but the lecture is about to start, so he continues up the stairs. Egashima is curious as to why his senior would be standing in front of the counter of the Academic Affairs Department. After attending the first class, he doesn't need to go through the lobby as his second-period class is in Building No. 4. Nevertheless, Egashima hurries there. Students are crisscrossing the lobby and chatting. His female senior is also sitting there holding a paperback in her hand. On seeing Egashima, she grins cheerfully.

"Did you buy this book?"

"*Kusa, makura?* – no, not yet."

Then she enquires about his friend.

"Oyama hasn't appeared yet. What is he taking this semester?"

"I don't know."

"Okay, never mind. Now listen, Egashima: I'm quitting college. I'm getting married later this month."

"You must be joking. That's a terrible joke!"

The senior becomes even more serious. She says that she is going to

marry a man older than her who is employed at her uncle's judicial scrivener office where she works. The uncle is also favorably disposed to his niece getting married to this employee colleague because the uncle has no heirs, and so he wants to leave the business to the two of them.

Egashima is shocked. Memories of those fun days with the female senior cascade through his head.

"Bijin-senpai, you're truly beautiful at heart, so your future husband must have fallen in love with you at first sight. I feel really happy for you."

"Come off it, Egashima. Not only my heart but my face also is beautiful!"

"Ah, oh yes of course."

"Where is your next class?"

"Room 423."

"I'm going to go home, so let's walk to Building 4 together."

The two arrive in front of Building 4. The lone ginkgo tree stands at the side of the road. A small tree shines brightly in the nightscape as if it were lit by all the lights of the university. It looks self-possessed, graceful, and like a tree with depth.

"I'll give you this book, *Kusamakura*. You'll be studying it in Prof Kamachi's class, and you should it read carefully. A river and a station appear at the end of the novel. I think it's the Shigenegi River. Some people call it the Nishiki River. The width of the two rivers is about the same, and if you go into town, you'll see willow trees on both river banks, and there's also an izakaya and a lumber yard. If you get off the boat at the foot of Nishiki Bridge, you can go straight to the station. I think the station is the Takase station because Soseki would always go through there whenever he traveled by train. On the other side of the station building, reeds were growing thick and rice fields spread out. That's why Soseki mentions such vegetation and calls it Yoshida's Station, to indicate a fertile area. It couldn't be a station on the Mt. Kinpo side. The main character in the story, the painter, comes over that mountain on his way to the inn. It's hard to know for sure which is the exact place. But, in my layman's opinion,

favoritism about place names creeps in. But it's interesting to read the novel while thinking about these things."

"Yes."

"Egashima, there is something else I want to say to you. You should go to university for four years. Two years is not enough. As you do have a job, graduating from Junior College might seem to be sufficient, less demanding, and appealing for you. But you should aim higher. Try to do your best. I think that education is a lifelong learning process. Acquiring knowledge can help us to make the correct choices in life when necessary. Even if huge changes occur, as is likely to, it is important to choose the right direction to go. I believe in you. Oh, there I go again! I'm sorry for being bossy right up to the end. You can come and visit me anytime."

"Yes, I would like to visit you sometime."

Egashima and his female senior part ways there and then. She turns around as she walks away and makes the usual gesture of raising her right hand as she continues toward the main gate. For a moment, Egashima stands there feeling stunned. Holding the book he has just received he rushes up the stairs of Building No. 4 to attend the first class in foreign languages, English. In Literature classes during the second semester, the focus is on summarizing and appreciating writings by Soseki under the course titled *'The World of Soseki's Literature.'* The novels covered include 'And Then,' 'The Gate,' 'Kokoro,' and 'The 210th Day.' There are no readings aloud by students. However, in 'Kusamakura,' the Professor frequently returns to the same lecture style as he had used in 'Sanshiro.' Ironically, 'Sanshiro,'' which begins in Autumn is read in the Spring semester, and 'Kusamakura,'' which is set at the beginning of Spring is being studied in Autumn. This approach intrigued Egashima. He decides to sit in the seat in which the female senior used to sit. In the next seat is a man some years older than him. Rumors about the female senior faded away as the days passed and very soon there was no gossip at all. It turns out that the man sitting next to Egashima works in a shoe store.

He talks at length about how busy he is mending the shoes of women who work in various types of eating establishments in the city. He says that life is tough for such women. They don't earn much, so many of them cannot afford to buy new shoes.

Egashima and the helpful female student never fail to greet each other. They exchange notebooks several times before their final exams. However, Egashima doesn't do well in that semester's final literature exam. He scores fifty-nine points, just one point short of a passing grade. Both Niina and Matsuo, his two colleagues, are surprised at his result. They sympathize with Egashima. So does Oyama.

11

Peeved at failing Literature by just one point, Egashima decides to take the course again the following academic year. He continues to devour Soseki's works as a second-timer. Even when he returned to his hometown for a few days during the Obon holidays he seemed to be reading most of the time. His family members were surprised at how much he had changed.

Egashima then discovers that, by immersing himself in the world of literature, he can find relief in different scenes as well as appreciate the emotions engendered by them. He also realized that strangely this absorption with literature enabled him to work extra hard in all sorts of trying conditions.

After the summer holidays of his sophomore year at university, September comes and with it the new semester. On the first Saturday night, Egashima invites the female student to a brass band concert in the Municipal Hall. His diary on the following day reads:

"Thank you for kindly putting up with my selfishness. The concert could not have been better. Even if it might not have been so interesting for you, it was an evening I'll never forget. To get the bus home, I deliberately chose the farthest bus stop from the Municipal Hall, walking through the Shintengai area and up Kamitori Street. For some reason, the bus stop that always feels far away seemed closer last night. Your feet must have hurt. Yet you cheerfully kept talking about many things. This makes you a person of more and more interest to me. Spending even a short time with you will be a lifetime memory for me. Thank you."

In early October, Egashima climbs a mountain in Kagoshima in the course of his work. His duty at the wireless communication relay station involves a long-term stay which means he is unable to attend university. He sends a cryptic message to one of his colleagues back at the base in Kumamoto, asking him to deliver the telegram by hand to the female student.

~ From the 100-meter altitude summit relay station in Kagoshima ~

Working in the scents of autumn surrounded by clouds is the epitome of happiness. Here it is similar to the summit of Mt. Kinpo in Kumamoto. The mountain has a lively atmosphere with people going on picnics. Everyone seems drenched in sweat after climbing up. They all say "hello" and I am having a great time. But since my duty here lasts until the 24th, I'm sending you this message over our wireless radio, along with the notice of my absence from classes.

Egashima returns from the mountains late at night on Saturday, the 24th. He participates in a sports festival held at the university the next day. The students of the Evening Division, who rarely get together during the daytime, enjoy a good time playing around under the soft autumn sun and a piercing blue sky. Egashima is able to exchange greetings with the female student for the first time in a while.

Soon after that sports event, the campus begins to experience the gradual approach of winter as witnessed by the trees starting to shed their leaves. Although it grows colder at night, the classrooms are equipped with steam heating systems which enable lectures to be carried out in a warm and comfortable atmosphere.

One evening, ten minutes before the start of his first-period class, Egashima enters Lecture Room 324 and sits down. As he is opening his foreign history textbook, the female student sits in a seat in front of him while chatting with her friends. As the two seats directly behind her were empty, she seemed quite near. Egashima observes her hair especially, which she has tied up with a yellow ribbon. He writes a note in the corner of his notebook:

"The nostalgia of one's youth is impossible to understand from remote adolescence. Looking back at my days of youth is akin to looking at the wind flowing around the distant moon. So now that I don't have the wistful longing of my youth, I can have a wonderful day every day. However, I must continue to give myself homework for tomorrow, so that the present doesn't end today."

Egashima finishes writing in his notebook and thinks about what *Bijin-senpai* might say.

"Normal! Normal!"

Egashima achieved a score of seventy-four points in the second-semester final exams in Literature.

12

"Egashima, this time you're doing it for real, but there is no need to be nervous. Be yourself, take control, and lead. In squad drills, it's important to have everyone in your unit complete the drills as you would like them to. If you're not satisfied, repeat the exercise as many times as you like. Give your commands slowly and clearly. The required results will follow. Lead from the heart. Have confidence in yourself. You can do it!"

"Yes, Sergeant Kashiwauchi, I'll do my best."

Tata-Tata-Tata, Tata—Tata

"Examinee Number 3. Leading Private Egashima. At the ready!"

"Start!"

"Fall in."

Tata-Tata-Tata, Tata—Tata

"Attention! From now on, this squad will be commanded by Leading Private Egashima. On your guard!"

"Squad Number…, Start. That's no good! Fall out. You're not getting it together. Let's do it again. Start!"

"1" "2" "3" "4" "5" "6" "7" "8" "9"

"These are the numbers for each individual squad member. From now on, we'll practice some steps at different intervals and some while marching."

The selection of examinees to become squad leader candidates continues.

Then, several months later.

Knock, knock.

"Come in,"

"Leading Private Egashima, I'm coming in."

"Egashima, I've received an official notice you've been designated as a successful candidate for the squad leader. Congratulations! Induction into your squad and admission to the academy will straddle the new school year, so your schedule and training are going to be a little irregular at first."

"I understand. Thank you for everything. I got this far thanks to your guidance as my company commander."

"What are you going to do about evening classes at the university? Do you want to submit a notice requesting a leave of absence?"

"Yes. It will mean a gap of two years, but I would like to continue to attend classes in the Evening Division at the university. Thank you so much for allowing me to study there until now."

Egashima goes to the university that same day. His third year of attending college is due to end within a few months. After he submits his application for a leave of absence from classes, his mind becomes very clear. As a candidate, he has to concentrate all his efforts on becoming a squad leader.

Egashima had nothing but feelings of gratitude for everything the university had given him. After saying farewell to the campus, Egashima used a public telephone to call his mother and tell her everything that had transpired that day.

Titles of Soseki's Works Interspersed in the Text		
Japanese Title	**English Title**	*Page*
Atatakai Yume	A Warm Dream	51
Botchan	Botchan	9
Buncho	The Caged Bird (A Bird)	44
Bungakuron	Theory of Literature	50
Garasu Do no Uchi	Inside the Glass Doors	40
Geshuku	The Boarding House	41
Gobijinso	The Field Poppy	26
Henka	The Change	73
Higan Sugi Made	To the Spring Equinox and Beyond	10
Kiri	Mists and Fogs	51
Kokoro	Kokoro (lit. Heart)	54
Kusamakura	The Three-Cornered World	9
Kōfu	The Miner	61
Kōjin	The Wayfarer	26
Meian	Light and Darkness	67
Michikusa	Grass on the Wayside	24
Mon	The Gate	73
Mukashi	The Past	66
Nihyakutōka	The 210th Day	5
Omoidasu Koto nado	Random Memories	12
Rondon Tō	The Tower of London	51
Sanshirō	Sanshirō	2
Sorekara	And Then	27
Tegami	A Letter	60
Wagahai wa Neko de aru	I Am a Cat	9
Watakushi no Kojin Shugi	My Individualism	59
Yume Jū-ya	Ten Nights of Dreams	34

Glossary of Japanese Words

akazake   red alcoholic drink peculiar to Kumamoto

bijin   a beautiful woman

ippon   a point awarded by judges in a competitive martial arts match

kiai   a short-spirited shout that is used to focus energy

kun   referring to men in general, male children, close male friends

nihyaku toka   the 210th day after the beginning of spring

nowaki   late autumn windstorm in the countryside

senpai   honorific for a mentor figure in some situation

The Author

Main Biographical Details

1947: Born in Tamana City, Kumamoto, Japan

1967: Graduated from Tamana High School

      Enlists in Ground Self-Defense Force (Telecommunication Unit)

1971: Graduated from Kumamoto Junior College (Social Studies)

      Transfers to Kumamoto University of Commerce (Faculty of Commerce)

1973: Drop out of Kumamoto University of Commerce

2001: Retired from Ground Self-Defense Force

2002: Employee of Sojo University

2014: Retired from Sojo University

At Present

Director of Tamana History Society

Journal "Tamana History" Editorial Committee Member

Member of Kumamoto Soseki Club

Member of Kumamoto Castle Commendation Society

Some Publications

"Seishun Showa Eigakan" (Showa Era Cinema in my Youth)

"Sebango 3" (Jersey Number 3)

"Soseki ni Shu Kotsu" (Autumn Bones in Soseki)

      (Kumanichi Publishing House)

"The actual scenery of the train station that appears in the final chapter of Natsume Soseki's novel "Kusamakura" (in Japanese)

      "Tamana History," No 103, February 2023

Translator's Afterword

Peter Flaherty

Egami Nobuyuki was born in Tamana, Kumamoto Prefecture two years after World War II finished. He belongs to the '*dankai-no-sedai*', where *dankai* means 'mass' and *sedai* means 'generation." Egami belongs to the first wave of the Baby Boomer Generation, those born during the three years of 1947 to 1949. The boomers had a huge impact in every area they were involved with, and their generation contributed much to the Japanese economy in achieving the spectacular growth that turned the country into an economic superpower as it recovered from the ashes of defeat in the war. Any proper interpretation of Japan must include a study of this demographical aspect, to get an objective understanding of the country's growth, the aging of society, population decline, and the future sociological significance of these factors.

Egami enlisted in the Ground Self-Defense Forces (SDF) after graduating from High School. He would have preferred to go to college, but his family circumstances did not permit such an option. In the SDF, Egami was assigned to the corps of engineers in the Multiple Wireless Communications Unit, and he specialized in telecommunications methods.

After being transferred to the army base in Kumamoto, Egami entered the night school of the Junior College of Kumamoto Commercial College, now part of Kumamoto Gakuen University. To graduate, apart from the number of academic credits necessary for a major in social studies, Ministry of Education regulations required that a student had also obtained a set number of credits in General Education subjects. What subjects to choose were optional. In his freshman year, Egami chose Japanese Literature, and Natsume Soseki's novels were the textbooks

84

set for the curriculum that year. Egami seems to have "fallen in love" with Soseki's literary works for various reasons, partly because of Prof. Kamachi who was the popular teacher of the course.

After university, Egami continued to serve his country through a career in the SDF. At the same time, he continued to pursue his deepening interest in literature and in particular in Soseki's works. The author also started to write and publish various essays and articles in Japanese.

After retiring from the SDF in 2001, Egami was employed by Sojo University as an engineer and he worked there until 2014. I met Egami-san at the university, where I was a teacher. My first impression of Egami was that of an affable, gregarious, kind, and energetic person with a good sense of humour. His interests varied a great deal from literature to movies and music. Egami heard that I, too, had an interest in Soseki and his works. One of the authors' favourite movies was the *Quiet Man* directed by John Ford and starring John Wayne and Maureen O'Hara. The romantic comedy-drama movie was filmed in Ireland and used many locations in Connemara, Co. Galway – the geographical part of the country that happens to be my native place. The thatched cottage used in the *Quiet Man* still stands there and is preserved to bear witness to the cinematic events happening in 1952, when I was five years of age. Such incidentals often became small-talk topics for the affable Egami-san and me when we occasionally met on campus.

Egami wrote this novella for two reasons. The first is to leave an account of the natural scenery and society when he was in his early twenties. The second purpose is to weave his experiences at that age into a "love story" that is recorded and told through a book in both Japanese and English.

When the author first asked me to do the English translation part, my initial

response was a refusal. However, as he gave me a signed complimentary copy of the original at the same time, I asked for some time to think over his request. Then on reading the Japanese version for the first time, I realized that my life overlapped with the author in several ways. We are the same age. I came from Tokyo to live in Kumamoto in 1974 shortly after Egami had left Kumamoto for Tokyo to do specialized training. A decade later, I began teaching as a part-time lecturer at the Night Division of the university Egami had attended and graduated from. I taught there for twenty-odd years. I immensely enjoyed teaching those "commuting working scholars", young adults who were very curious about me and what kept me going. A question I was frequently asked was "Why are you still here?" Very often tired students would ask me other questions that were more related to sharing musings on the vicissitudes of life rather than studying the rudiments of the English language.

On reading Egami's version of the place I had come to five decades earlier, I realized that there had been so much I was blind to and ignorant of at the time. I had learned much and grown from my interactions with the students, especially the working students in the Evening Division. When Egami-san plaintively asked me again to do the translation, I realized it would be a good opportunity to take a re-look at a crucial period of my life. I also realized that I could do so from hindsight – rather than as a teacher and when I had to evaluate students' performance to give or deny academic credits. Those wonderful young adults were eager to deepen their knowledge and improve the quality of their lives. In the hustle and bustle of a full classroom, at times it was easy to forget the individuality of each person and their paramount reality of trying to make a living in existential circumstances that could be very trying.

In conclusion, I enjoyed doing the translation while resurrecting myriad

memories of people and events. Finally, I would like to express my gratitude to Egami-san for sharing one part of his life journey with me. Through this translation, I hope others will also get an insight into a place and once upon a time in Japan.